"Who has the combination to the safe?" Andrew asked

Jennifer stood up. "Only Matt and I," she answered emphatically, proud of their security.

"Matt was with me, so he couldn't have been stealing those sketches. That leaves only one other person who could have opened the safe."

"What...what are you implying?" she gasped.

He smiled, a slow lingering smile. "You had me fooled," he drawled, "but I must admit your act was very convincing. You don't look like a thief, Jennifer, but then thieves seldom do."

"Just what are you saying?" she begged again.

"I'm saying the obvious," Andrew answered slowly, his eyes raking her face with disgust, "and the obvious is...you're guilty!"

Books by Rosemary Badger

HARLEQUIN ROMANCE
2617—CORPORATE LADY
2629—A GIRL CALLED ANDY
2695—A TIME OF DECEPTION

These books may be available at your local bookseller.

Don't miss any of our special offers. Write to us at the following address for information on our newest releases.

Harlequin Reader Service
P.O. Box 52040, Phoenix, AZ 85072-2040
Canadian address: P.O. Box 2800, Postal Station A,
5170 Yonge St., Willowdale, Ont. M2N 6J3

A Time
of Deception

Rosemary Badger

Harlequin Books

TORONTO • NEW YORK • LONDON
AMSTERDAM • PARIS • SYDNEY • HAMBURG
STOCKHOLM • ATHENS • TOKYO • MILAN

Original hardcover edition published in 1984
by Mills & Boon Limited

ISBN 0-373-02695-1

Harlequin Romance first edition June 1985

CHAPTER ONE

THE ringing shattered her slumber. Jennifer Sloane rolled on to her side and let the telephone ring several more times, before she finally answered it.

'Hullo,' she answered sleepily, her green eyes cloudy from sleep as she checked the time on her little alarm clock. Barely eight o'clock.

'Jennifer!' For God's sake, where have you been? I've been trying to reach you for the past half hour.' Matt Bloomfield's voice crackled in her ear. Jennifer groaned and fell back on to her pillow, her silky blonde hair spreading like a fan around her head.

'I've been sleeping, Matt,' she answered, a slender hand moving up to stifle a yawn. 'You told me to take the day off, remember? You were feeling guilty about the twelve-hour days I've been working all this week and thought I looked rather tired. "Exhausted", was the word I think you used last night when . . .'

'Cut the sarcasm,' Matt interrupted sharply. 'I know what I said, but I need you here. Now!'

Jennifer sat up in bed, all traces of sleep completely gone. 'What is it, Matt?' she asked softly, her knuckles white as she gripped the phone. 'Not more of the same?'

''Fraid so,' answered Matt, and Jennifer pictured him at his desk, a rough hand moving restlessly through the thinning grey hair. 'Our phantom raider has struck again!'

The phone became heavy in her hand and she had to lick her lips before she was able to ask: 'Which campaign?'

'Corser Car Products.' There was a dry chuckle and she could hear the pages of a magazine turning before Matt continued, 'Would you believe all our jingles have been used to describe a brand of dishwashing detergent that I've never heard of?'

Jennifer could believe it all right. For the past few months practically every small campaign the Adam Thorpe Advertising Agency had worked on had been stolen from the agency to appear in cheap, third-rate magazines. The Corser Car Products represented weeks of hard work and was to be stretched over a two-week period of prime advertising time on television, radio and with coverage in leading newspapers and magazines.

The entire agency had been involved in this campaign and the Corser Car Products, while not their largest account, was one of their biggest and probably their most difficult campaign to work on. Labels had had to be designed for the Corser's group of sixteen products. Also the agency had had to come up with something 'startingly new and eye-catching', to quote the head of the Corser advertising department, if they hoped to be able to compete with their ever-increasing number of competitors. Now all these brilliant ideas, the hard work, the sweat and sometimes the tears, had been wasted on some cheap brand of detergent that no one had ever heard of, in a magazine that no one bothered to buy.

Apart from a few minor alterations, the entire campaign had been approved and accepted by the Corser Group. Now, Jennifer knew, the campaign would have to be scrapped, excuses made to their client and a whole new campaign set out. If the Corser group decided to take their business elsewhere, which was a strong possibility, there would be a loss, not only financially but on the reliability and dependability which had been the foundation the Adam Thorpe Advertising Agency had built its reputation on and which had helped make them the leading advertising company in Sydney.

If the Corser Group stayed with them, then a fresh campaign would need to be ready within ten days to correspond with television and radio schedules which had been booked months in advance. Jennifer didn't allow her thoughts to take her further. She knew, just as Matt knew, just as every member of the staff would know, that if the Corser Group took their business away, word would spread like wildfire that the Thorpe Agency had lost its touch and big companies would avoid them like the plague. There would be no new clients and their established clientele would dwindle to extinction. There was superstition in big business. No one liked the smell of a loser!

'Does the old man know?' Jennifer asked now. 'The old man' was Adam Thorpe, founder of the Agency, and in the four years Jennifer had worked at the agency, she had never heard him referred to as anything else but 'the old man'. It was an expression used with great respect and affection, for Adam Thorpe was a man in his late seventies and rarely paid a visit to the agency. Jennifer had only met him three times—the day she was hired, fresh from design school and twice after that, when he had held brief meetings. But she had often times wished she had known him in his heyday, for she had listened to many stories from Matt, recounting times when Adam Thorpe was a man to be reckoned with. From these stories, Jennifer also guessed how much Matt, himself close to retirement age, missed the leadership of the old man.

'No, he hasn't been told,' Matt admitted. 'We got through the others, we'll get through this one as well.'

'But this one's different, Matt,' argued Jennifer. 'It's bigger and more complicated. We can't continue feeding this thief. He's got to be stopped. I'm sure if you would only tell the old man what's going on, he would insist we contact the police.'

'The police!' Matt snorted in disgust. 'I've told you before, Jennifer, that the police are out of the question. If word of this ever got around, we'd be out in the streets. People pay us top money for originality. How long do you think we'd last if even one client found out that we have a sneak thief in our midst?' It wasn't really a question and Jennifer knew she wasn't expected to answer. She and Matt had had this argument countless times before now. But it was the first time either one had admitted that the thief could very well be a member of the staff. It was a logical conclusion, but one that wasn't very pretty.

'Well, something has got to be done, Matt,' she insisted. 'Our thief tried us out with small game, probably to test us. When we did nothing, he obviously took it as a green light, going from small accounts to much bigger ones like the Corser Car Products. We're all overworked as it is, Matt. We can't continue indefinitely creating new stuff to replace what's been stolen. Besides,' she added disparagingly, 'one of these times we're going to miss seeing one of our campaigns in those shoddy magazines. We can't police *every* magazine and circular that goes out, Matt. Then it will appear as if *we* stole our ideas from *them*!'

You're right, Jen,' Matt conceded, and it saddened her to hear the tiredness and disappointment in his voice. He continued softly, no brusqueness in his tone now, 'You know, Jen, I've been in this business for almost as long as I can remember and nothing like this has ever happened before. Quite frankly, I just don't know what to do.' There was a slight pause and then he said, 'To add insult to injury, the old man's son is in town. He rang earlier. He wants to hold a staff meeting at one o'clock. What can we tell him?'

Jennifer's heart skipped a beat. The old man's son! She had met him once . . .

'We haven't a choice, Matt. We must tell him everything. He'll know what to do!'

Now why had she said that? she wondered a few minutes later as she turned the taps for her shower. The old man's son . . . Andrew Thorpe. It was true, she had met him once. Or rather, it was more as if she had been in his presence once! She smiled as she lathered her long-limbed body with the sweet-smelling soap, remembering the time, almost four years ago now, when she had met Andrew Thorpe.

Barely nineteen years old and fresh from design school, she had sat with the other hopeful applicants, each of them with their art portfolios held carefully on their laps. waiting to be interviewed by the old man. To win a position with the Adam Thorpe Advertising Agency was, to an art graduate, what it would be to a mathematician to work with Einstein. Only the best would be hired. Only the most creative would remain.

The old man screened his applicants carefully, before any interviews took place. This was a well-known fact and each of the five applicants outside the old man's office knew their work must be equal, but that a personal quality, none of them knew what would either win them a position or lose it for them.

When it was Jennifer's turn, she had exchanged her seat in the small reception area outside the old man's office, to take the one indicated directly in front of the old man's desk. The old man was seated, his snow-white hair thick and luxurious as it fell in untidy tendrils over his shirt collar. Piercing black eyes scrutinised her from beneath thick white brows. She had decided he was the most beautiful creature she had ever seen and immediately forgot all the dreadful stories of how he devoured artists the way a dog devours a bone.

She might have relaxed if it hadn't been for the much younger man standing by the window in the old man's office. She had known, even before Andrew Thorpe was introduced to her, that he must be the old man's son. He was dressed casually, a white sports shirt opened at the neck to reveal tanned skin and topped by a lightweight tweed sports jacket. One hand was thrust into a pocket of beige trousers. The same piercing black eyes watched her from beneath thick black brows. But whereas his father possessed an air of gentleness, typical of an artist, Andrew Thorpe appeared tough, almost menacing as he stood there by the window watching her. There was an air of bored arrogance about him, which completely unsettled her, robbing her of the little bit of confidence she had managed to pysche herself into for the sole purpose of this interview.

Andrew's gaze had settled on her portfolio and she saw the amusement flicker in his eyes as though it were some kind of joke that she should have to bare all that which had come from her heart.

The old man had stood when she had entered his office and after introducing himself, had introduced his son. She had murmured her acknowledgments before taking her seat, feeling extremely young, foolish and nervous in the face of these two aristocratic lions.

Her hair had been much longer then, she remembered, and she had worn it straight down her back. She smiled now at her reflection. Her hair was a bit darker and she no longer wore it straight. Still very blonde, her hair was now shoulder-length and she had it trimmed regularly to maintain its soft curve. As she applied make-up sparingly, she remembered that at the time of her interview she had worn no make-up at all. She also remembered that Andrew Thorpe had called her 'Cinderella'.

The old man had reached for her portfolio, but for some unaccountable reason Jennifer had held back, clutching her portfolio to her chest. Andrew had moved from the window and crossed over to where she sat. 'Come on, little Cinderella,' he had said, gently prying the portfolio from her clenched fingers. 'Let's see if the glass slipper fits!'

Jennifer had watched him go through her work, her tongue dry against the roof of her mouth. Andrew had flicked through the pages, stopping now and then to examine a particular piece in more detail. At these times, she had only started breathing when the dark hands holding her works moved on again. Several times he had looked at her, black eyes boring into green, giving her the distinct impression that he was exploring her soul. Andrew had finally handed her portfolio over to his father and taken his place again by the window, his back to both her and the old man. Jennifer felt as if all her energy had been sapped from her. As far as she was concerned, the interview was over. She no longer cared if the old man liked her work; it had been enough that Andrew had. And she *knew* Andrew had liked her work. She *knew* it! A few days later the old man had rung and told her to start work the following Monday.

Jennifer had never seen Andrew again. When

she found out that Andrew didn't work at the Agency, her disappointment was so keen that she almost gave up her job. But she had managed to get a grip on herself, chastising herself for her foolishness. After all, she told herself, Andrew was much older than her, perhaps by as much as ten years. He was a man, while she was merely a girl. But this fact didn't prevent her devouring any office gossip that centred on the old man's son. Jennifer learned from others that Andrew had been a bit of a rogue, refusing to enter his father's business, preferring instead to make it on his own. Equipped with an engineering degree, he had struck out for Europe. Within a few short years, according to the office gossips, he had accumulated mass fortunes by purchasing old run-down warehouses and converting them into factories to manufacture machinery of his own designs. Jennifer had supplemented this information with titbits from the social pages whenever Andrew was in Sydney. His good looks and obvious wealth seemed to provide him with a never-ending source of beautiful women. Once, although Jennifer would never admit it even under torture, she had learned through the gossip columns that Andrew Thorpe was to attend an opera at the Sydney Opera House. She had stood in line for five solid hours to purchase a ticket to the same opera. Then the line began dispersing in front of her and people became angry. 'What is it?' she had asked to a disgruntled passer-by. 'They've sold the last ticket!' was the mumbled reply. After that, she had forced herself to put Andrew out of her mind.

Now, after all this time, she was to meet him again. Would he remember her? she wondered. Of course he wouldn't. She wasn't the same shy little girl she had been four years ago. As she studied her face in the mirror, she realised she didn't even look the same. She had filled out, her style of clothing was much different and even her hair was a different colour. But the biggest change was in her personality. She was now very much her own person, self-assured and confident. The 'Cinderella' image had been lost about the same time she had forced Andrew from her mind.

Slipping into a pale blue cotton bathrobe, Jennifer stepped on to the tiled balcony off her bedroom. She had purchased this unit two years ago, and one of the deciding factors had been the view. Overlooking Manly harbour, a Sydney suburb, the scene was forever changing. Small sailing craft dominated the green waters of the Pacific Ocean. Hydrofoils skimmed across the waters and the huge Manly ferries chugged back and forth, taxiing people between Sydney and Manly.

From her balcony she could see the beginnings of the Sydney scene, the rise of skyscrapers jutting into the clear blue skies. Below, on the sandy beach, children frolicked under the watchful eyes of young mothers. Jennifer sighed and walked back to her bedroom. She had planned to spend the morning at the beach, soak up the sun, go swimming.

She dressed with extreme care, refusing to admit she was dressing for Andrew. From her wardrobe she had selected a hunter green dress which, she knew, set off her hair and eyes to perfection. Her excitement increased by the second and for once, the Agency with its problems, was far from her mind. She knew, as she put the final touches to her make-up, that she hadn't, after all, put Andrew from her mind. He had always been there, and now, finally, she was to meet him again.

As was her custom, Jennifer took the hydrofoil into Sydney. The ride lasted for twelve minutes and was an invigorating start to her day. If she took her car, she would be at least an hour in the traffic before she reached the Agency. Then there was always the problem about parking.

Matt was waiting for her when she arrived at work. She smiled when she saw him. Poor old Matt, she thought, this business with the thief had really got to him. Then, immediately, she had pangs of guilt. The thief had got to her as well, but it had also provided the chance to keep Andrew here. Jennifer had no doubt whatsoever, that Andrew would get to the bottom of the problem, stalk out the thief and bring him to justice. He would save the Agency and they could all get back to business. After that? She didn't dare think!

'You jolly well took your time getting here,' Matt growled his greeting. 'What did you do? Walk?

Jennifer tucked her arm in his and together they strolled towards the lift which would take them to the third floor and to their suite of offices. 'Now, Matt,' she smiled, 'it's been less than an hour since I spoke to you on the phone. Don't be such an old grouch—it frightens me.'

Matt patted her hand and chuckled. 'You've never been afraid of me and you now it! Serves me right, though, I've always been soft where you're concerned.'

'Soft! You bully me every chance you get. You snarl and growl like an old bear,' she laughed.

He guided her into the lift. 'You're in especially high spirits today ... considering.'

She knew what he meant and guilt swept over her. 'It doesn't do any good worrying all the time, Matt,' she defended. 'Besides, I feel everything will turn out fine.'

'You have that much faith in Andrew, do you?' he asked casually.

Jennifer shot him a look, but he was watching the lights above him, ticking off the floors.

'Well, yes, Matt, actually I have. Andrew Thorpe isn't directly involved with the Agency the way we are. The thief has probably left clues, which we've been too close to see. Andrew will be able to view the situation objectively, see things from a different slant.'

'I wish he didn't have to know, all the same,' Matt sighed. 'He won't like it.'

None of us *likes* it, Matt, but it's good that we'll be getting some help.' The lift came to a halt on the third floor and as Matt and Jennifer stepped out, Jennifer asked:

'What's he like, Matt? Andrew, I mean. Do ... do you know him at all?'

'Know him?' Matt chuckled. 'I've known Andrew Thorpe all his life. He's much like his father was at that age. Domineering, pigheaded—

you name it, the Thorpes have it!' He smiled down at her. 'But you've met him. You told me once that he sat in on your interview with the old man.'

'Yes, that's right,' Jennifer murmured, hoping her face wasn't as red as it felt. 'Meeting someone briefly isn't knowing them, though.' She paused before continuing. 'Still, there was something about Andrew Thorpe which made me feel he was the man for any job. I feel he's the right man for this job, Matt, and I'm glad he's in town. It saves us from having to worry the old man with this whole sordid mess.'

The Thorpe Advertising Agency occupied three floors. On the third floor, where Jennifer and Matt had their suite of offices, was a small reception area, luxuriously outfitted with deep-cushioned sofas and chairs. Original oil paintings lined the cream-coloured walls. Royal blue carpeting covered the floors and complemented pale blue furnishings. There was a gleaming rosewood desk which faced the door and was to the left of Jennifer's office. Matt's office was a bit further down and a reading table separated his office door from Jennifer's.

Cheryle Carpenter, a pretty young brunette, looked up from her typing where she sat at the rosewood desk when Jennifer and Matt entered. Matt had hired Cheryle twelve months ago and had once confided to Jennifer that he hired her because her dark hair offered a contrast to the cream-coloured walls! Jennifer had looked over Cheryle's application and had been suitably impressed with her record of employment. Both

Jennifer and Matt greatly appreciated her skills. Cheryle kept them organised, was discreet, prompt, and never forgot to change the water in the various vases which housed the fresh carnations Matt held a passion for.

'Oh, Miss Sloane,' she greeted Jennifer, 'I understood you weren't coming in today.'

'You understood correctly, Cheryle, but unfortunately ol' Scrooge here,' and Jennifer looked fondly towards Matt, 'took back his offer of a well-earned rest and ordered me back to the saltmines.' Jennifer stopped at Cheryle's desk and looked for her mail. Matt continued on to his office, where she would join him later to thrash out the day's problems.

'I've already sorted the mail, Miss Sloane,' Cheryle said. 'There wasn't anything for you to handle directly, so I've passed it on through the usual channels.'

'Thank you, Cheryle. I suspect I'll be busy in Matt's office most of the morning. There's a meeting scheduled for one o'clock, but apart from that, I have nothing urgent planned. If Mr Livingston rings, tell him I'll meet him at our usual place at seven o'clock.'

'Very well, Miss Sloane,' answered Cheryle, jotting down what Jennifer had told her in her notebook. 'This meeting at one o'clock—I haven't written it in the diary. Is it an impromptu meeting with staff heads, or has something urgent come up?'

'All our meetings tend to be "urgent", Cheryle,' Jennifer half laughed, as she made her way across the reception area to her own office. 'With Matt at the helm, and with what's been going on here lately, red lights are always flashing, or so it seems.'

Seated at her desk, Jennifer made several phone calls, arranging meetings with clients. Next she dictated letters into the dictaphone which Cheryle would type up later and then got out files which contained all the campaigns which had been pilfered. From the bottom drawer of her filing cabinet she dragged out the various magazines and circulars their campaigns had appeared in and set about matching them with their corresponding files.

A buzzer sounded and she picked up her phone to hear Cheryle's voice on the other end. 'Sorry to disturb you, Miss Sloane, but Mr Livingston insists on speaking with you.'

'Very well, Cheryle, put him through.' Almost immediately Kevin's voice came across the wire.

'What's the idea giving your secretary messages to pass on to me? Don't tell me you're too busy to spend a few minutes talking to the man who wants to marry you!'

Jennifer smiled into the mouthpiece. 'Sorry, Kevin, but I'm busy.' Her eyes rested on the files spread across her desk. 'I've got an important meeting scheduled for one o'clock and there's a lot that needs to be prepared.'

'You always seem to have important meetings,' he laughed. 'There always seems to be something earth-shattering going on at that place. What is it this time?'

'We've had another campaign stolen,' she told him. 'A much bigger, more important one this time.'

'Really?'

'Yes, really. This thing has really got out of hand, Kevin.'

'Does your boss still insist on handling it himself, or do you think, now, he'll go to the police?'

Jennifer sighed. Kevin had once worked with Matt and knew what she was up against.

'No, he still feels the same. You know what Matt's like—once he gets an idea into his mind, it's hard to dissuade him. He thinks going to the police would only result in bad publicity.'

'He's probably right, Jennifer. Reporters lurk around police stations. You'd get publicity, all right.'

'Well, enough of my problems. How's your day going, Kevin?'

'Couldn't be better. Three sales came through today. Just like my pappy always said,' he joked, 'there's no business like the real estate business.' There was the sound of muffled voices at Kevin's end and Jennifer had to wait before he came on the line again. 'Sorry about that,' he said. 'Another client has just come in, looking to buy a house. I'll have to go now, Jen. I only rang to remind you it's Friday. Meet you at our usual place tonight? Around seven?'

'Yes, see you, Kevin and good luck with your sale.'

Jennifer smiled as she placed the phone on its

receiver. Kevin always managed to spruce up her spirits. She had been dating him now for almost two years, and while their relationship had never developed into anything deep, despite Kevin's teasing that they would one day marry, they were good friends and had followed a ritual of meeting for dinner each Friday evening after work.

Matt came into her office and frowned when he saw the files spread across her desk. 'What are you doing?' he asked.

'Getting these ready for Andrew Thorpe,' Jennifer answered. 'I thought we agreed we should tell . . . and show . . . him everything.'

He shook his head. 'I've changed my mind,' he said, 'and the others agree with me. Unless Andrew asks directly, and there's no reason why he should, we won't tell him anything about the thefts. He'll only be in town for a week or so anyway, so there wouldn't be enough time for him to solve anything for us. We'll handle it by ourselves.'

Jennifer felt Matt was making a big mistake, but she supposed he had reasons of his own for not wanting to take Andrew Thorpe into his confidence. As she put the files away and shut the drawer, however, she couldn't help feeling she was taking part in a conspiracy. Andrew Thorpe had a right to know what was going on. As Matt turned and left her office, a little of the respect she held for him left with him.

At twelve-thirty, she took her place at the gleaming mahogany table in the boardroom. The meeting with Andrew was scheduled for one o'clock, but already all the concerned staff members were present, each with his briefcase in front of him, toying with papers they had brought for discussions with Andrew. No one spoke. It was as if they were all suddenly strangers, and a deep uneasiness prevailed in the room.

At precisely one o'clock, Andrew Thorpe strolled into the boardroom, and all paper rustling came to an immediate halt!

CHAPTER TWO

THE atmosphere in the boardroom was electric as
Andrew, dressed in a dark grey business suit,
greeted his father's staff. Only Matt, who had
known Andrew all his life, responded with any
warmth. The others were reserved, and Jennifer
wondered if Andrew could sense their fear.

Andrew's piercing black eyes settled briefly on
Jennifer, causing her heart to race dangerously. He
seemed mildly surprised that a woman should be
sitting in on a boardroom meeting. Apart from
that, there was no flicker of recognition, and
Jennifer bit back her disappointment.

Andrew had carried in several files and now
spread them on the highly polished table. He
wasted no time getting down to business,
dispensing with matters quickly and efficiently. It
was easy to see why he was a highly successful
business man and his knowledge of his father's
business was astounding, but Jennifer wasn't really
surprised. Matt had told her that Andrew had
worked at the agency during school vacations and
as a little boy spent most of his time following his
father and Matt around the place.

With the last of the business dispensed with,
Andrew closed the files and placed them in a neat
pile in the centre of the table. Then he stood back
and looked at each of them in turn.

He was well over six feet tall, his dark grey business suit seemed to emphasise not only his height, but also the lean powerfulness of his figure. His black eyes had narrowed shrewdly in the sternly handsome face and the well-cut, sensual mouth spread into a mocking smile.

'There's trouble,' he said softly, his black gaze settling on Jennifer. 'Perhaps the young lady with the green eyes can tell me what it is.'

Jennifer flushed, not only because Andrew had called her 'green eyes' but also because he had sensed they were hiding something from him. Jennifer felt her colleagues stiffen around her and despite the warning glance Matt shot her, she knew there would be no point in hiding anything from Andrew Thorpe. He was not the type of man who would settle for the scraps of information they had planned on giving him.

She squared her shoulders and looked directly at Andrew, her green eyes not wavering under the potent force of his own black ones. 'My name happens to be Jennifer Sloane,' she said quietly. 'I've been working at the Adam Thorpe Advertising Agency for almost four years and I'm Matt's assistant.' Up till now, there hadn't been any reason for her to speak. When she stole a glance at Matt, Matt seemed surprised by her boldness. But she wanted Andrew to know that she was an important member of the agency and that hard work not the fact that she had green eyes and was female, had brought her to her present level.

Andrew's eyes glittered with amusement. 'Very

well, Cinderella. Now that you've got that off your chest, perhaps you can brief me on what's going on around here.' His eyes moved lazily around the table and Jennifer saw that no one, not even Matt, could look him in the eye. His gaze returned to her. 'Ready, Cinderella?' he asked, and there was no mistaking the teasing quality in his voice. Jennnifer knew he was letting her know he would damned well call her anything he liked! What he didn't know was that she was secretly pleased that he had remembered about Cinderella.

'You've guessed we've been experiencing a bit of trouble,' she began, deciding it would be wise to give it to him straight. 'For the past few months, some of our campaigns have been stolen. These campaigns have been used to advertise products not associated with any of our clients.'

A hushed silence followed her words. Jennifer looked across at Matt. He was staring down at his hands, a glum expression on his face. Helplessly, she looked up at Andrew, realising for the first time that Matt would be held responsible for this breach in security. Since the old man had gone into almost total retirement, the running of the agency had been placed primarily into Matt's hands.

But while there was no condemnation in Andrew's eyes, neither was there sympathy.

'You're telling me' he drawled, 'that this has been going on for months without the police tracking down the culprit?'

He was looking at Jennifer and she knew he expected her to answer. It was almost as though he had forgotten there were others sitting around the table. He had placed her in the hot seat.

'Well, actually,' she swallowed hard, painfully aware of Matt across from her, 'actually, we thought it best not to notify the police.'

He laughed, but there was no humour in it and the sound chilled her heart.

'Espionage has been going on for months and you thought it *best* not to notify the police?' he asked incredulously.

Jennifer felt anger rising in her throat and when she spoke she was amazed that she managed to sound so calm. 'Yes,' she answered matter-of-factly, 'that's exactly what we did think. We didn't want adverse publicity.'

Andrew drew in his breath and then let it out on a long sigh. 'All right,' he said, still ignoring the others in the room, concentrating solely on Jennifer. 'You decided against the police. What measures *did* you take?'

'Measures?' she asked dumbly. 'What do you mean?'

His dry smile was infuriatingly mocking. 'Steps! What steps did you take to catch your thief?' His tone indicated that he considered himself to be dealing with a not very bright two-year-old. Hot colour seared Jennifer's cheeks.

'Why, the usual,' she answered. 'We lock up at night; we make certain nothing is left lying around, which might end up in the wrong hands, we . . .'

'Those are *preventive* measures,' he cut in, rudely too, she thought. 'I've asked for information on what's been done to apprehend your thief. If you decided against the police, you must have had a better plan, although obviously it hasn't worked if after six months the thief is still at large.'

His arrogance amazed her. 'I'll have you know, Mr Andrew Thorpe, that we've been flat out just keeping up with our work load. None of us claims to be Sherlock Holmes, but we've all done our best to outsmart the thief. Most of us have been working twelve and fourteen hours a day to keep this business afloat. We've held meetings ... endless meetings ... trying to decide on a course of action ...'

'Well,' prompted Andrew, when it appeared she wasn't about to continue, 'what course of action, if any, did you decide upon?'

She stole a look at Matt. His face was a sickly ashen colour. Her heart went out to him.

'Actually, it was Matt who decided what we must do,' she said. 'Matt had already put on an extra security guard and when that didn't work and when he heard you were in town, he decided the wisest thing would be to tell you. Matt felt,' she rushed on, 'that you would be in a better position to see things, take a more objective view than we ever could. Matt feels confident you'll catch the thief. We all do,' she added stoutly, nodding her head.

Andrew's black eyes probed her face and she lowered her eyes so that he would not see she was lying about Matt. When she raised her eyes, finally, it was to see he was smiling at her—a deeply sensuous smile that left no doubt to what his thoughts were! Blushing deeply, she again averted her head, this time to look at Matt, who gave her a grateful look.

He rose to his feet, brushing a hand tiredly through his thinning hair. He had caught the smile Andrew had bestowed on Jennifer, but it was only from a side view. The deep sensuality and the message from the coal black eyes had been for Jennifer alone and not meant for Matt or anyone else to see or to interpret. Matt thought the smile meant Andrew guessed Jennifer was covering for him. Andrew had guessed that all right, but it hadn't disturbed him the way Matt thought it might. Now Matt spoke: 'The truth of the matter, Andrew, is ... we're scared. We've taken what precautions we could, but none of them have worked. This ... this person who is stealing our ideas, in some cases whole campaigns, has got us hoodwinked.' He spread his hands in a hopeless gesture of despair. 'Perhaps Jennifer is right ... if you've got the time, Andrew, we would appreciate your help. Objectivity, as Jennifer has suggested, just might be the key.'

Matt sat down and the other members of the staff murmured their approval, looking expectantly at Andrew. Jennifer felt her colleagues relaxing around her, and it wasn't difficult to guess why. Matt was their boss, but Andrew was the old man's son. It was far wiser to be on the side of a man with Andrew's formidable qualities, than against him. They looked upon Andrew now as their leader.

Throughout the meeting, Andrew had remained

standing. Now he sat on the edge of the table, long legs bent at the knees. He thoughtfully probed his chin, as he looked down at his shoes. No one spoke. Finally he looked up and, as he had done before, looking at each of them in turn.

'From what you've told me,' he drawled, 'it appears obvious that it's an inside job!'

There were gasps of protest, but Andrew merely smiled. His smile was indulgent, as though they were little more than children with not a brain to spare among themselves.

'Has to be,' he continued in that same drawl. 'Your thief would have to know *in advance* which campaigns are being planned. When he knows this, he finds a suitable market, then matches his product to fit your campaign and begins advertising. You're doing all the work, while he sits back and reaps the benefits.' Andrew gave Jennifer a meaningful look. 'Elementary, my dear Watson. Elementary!'

The brute was enjoying himself, Jennifer knew, but despite this there was open admiration on her face as she stared at him. It *was* elementary, but none of them had seen it. She looked around at the others and saw they thought the same. Someone now working at the Thorpe Advertising Agency was a thief.

Excited babbling followed, which gradually diminished into shocked disbelief. It couldn't be— but then, one by one, each accepted the inevitable. It had to be. There was no other explanation. Uneasiness followed the excitement.

A thought occurred to Jennifer and she drew her

fine brows into a frown. Andrew glanced at her, noticing the perplexity on her face. 'You don't agree with my theory, Jennifer?' he asked. 'Or perhaps you have something you would like to add.'

She flicked back the golden halo of her hair. Green eyes flashed as she looked at Andrew and a flush crept into her cheeks. She smiled. Would anyone dare *dis*agree with him? she thought. She turned her glance from Andrew and spoke to the others, deliberately ignoring him. 'Perhaps we shouldn't be too hasty in assuming our thief works here at the agency. After all,' she continued, 'a lot of our work is passed to outsiders. Binding, for instance ... we have several binders scattered throughout the city, and then there's the photographers. Sometimes it's not always possible to use our own, and in the case of the Corser Car Products, we did use a freelance photographer with some of our outdoor shots.'

She swung back to Andrew, a look of triumph in her eyes. Her colleagues were nodding and smiling. The thief was probably someone from outside.

'I think,' Andrew replied casually, his black eyes alight with amusement as he studied Jennifer's face, 'that before we start checking in someone else's backyard, we explore our own territory first.' He stood up from where he was perched at the table's edge and shrugged out of his jacket, placing the garment on the back of a chair. Next, he loosened his tie and then rolled up his sleeves, the white of the shirt in sharp contrast against the tanned hue of muscular forearms. Jennifer had followed his movements, wondering if he was going to undress entirely! She had attended several boardroom meetings, and while most of the men removed their jackets and loosened their ties in their own offices, none of them would ever dream of doing it at a boardroom meeting.

'Go back to your sections,' he ordered them, 'and compile lists of those who are directly involved with sales campaigns. Bring your lists back here, where we'll go through them one by one. Let's hope a pattern will emerge and we'll then have a "short list" of potential thieves.'

He sat down at the gleaming table and began scribbling notes in one of his files. One by one the staff left the boardroom. It was obvious they had been dismissed. Jennifer decided she had never known anyone quite so rude. She left with the others, biting back what she would dearly have loved to say to him.

Outside the boardroom, Matt turned to Jennifer. 'I have a splitting headache,' he told her. 'You grab the files from your office and I'll meet you back here. I'm going to grab a few aspirins from the infirmary.'

Cheryle was typing the letters Jennifer had put on the dictating machine. She looked up from her work when Jennifer entered the small reception room. 'Meeting over, Miss Sloane?' she smiled.

'No, Cheryle, it's barely begun! I'm just here to pick up some files.'

In her office, Jennifer ran a comb through her hair and touched up her lipstick, using the little mirror in the cupboard that housed an extra pair of shoes, a cardigan, an umbrella and a few other odds and ends which saw her through any number of emergencies.

From her filing cabinet, she removed the files and magazines she had planned to take to the boardroom meeting, in the first place. It made an awkward bundle in her arms and she had to struggle with the door, before opening it.

Cheryle was on the telephone, and when Jennifer caught her eye, raising her brow inquisitively, she shook her head. Placing her hand over the mouthpiece, she told Jennifer, 'It's nothing important, Miss Sloane. I can handle it.'

'Good,' smiled Jennifer, then added, 'If something urgent comes up, put the call through to the boardroom. 'I'll take it there.'

She carried her bundle down the carpeted corridor leading to the boardroom. The door was closed and she balanced the bundle on one bent knee as she struggled with the knob. Almost immediately, the door was flung open and she would have lost her balance if Andrew hadn't caught her. The files fell to the floor and the magazines dropped beside them. Andrew kicked them in, his arms still around her, as he guided her inside the door, kicking it shut behind them.

Breathlessly, she looked up at him, aware of her heart beating crazily in her chest. Even with her high heels and as tall as she was, the top of her head barely reached his chin. Her arms were folded up against his chest and she could feel the stretch of muscles against the palms of her hands. He smiled down at her, teeth flashing white against darkly sensuous lips. She struggled against him, but her efforts were futile against the strength of his hold and only served to cause him to tighten his grip.

'Let me go!' she hissed, drawing back her head to glare at him wildly, her green eyes flashing.

In answer he merely removed his hands from her back to clasp both her hands, forcing them around his neck. Then he slid his arms around her again, moulding her slender young body against the hard contours of his own. His hands possessed her with an intimacy she had never known, and she quivered against him, a deep cry tearing from her throat when she felt him squeezing her buttocks, pressing her against him. His hands never stopped and his eyes never left her face. When finally she moaned and closed her eyes, his mouth came crashing down on hers, forcing her lips apart, beginning an exploration that was every bit as thorough as his hands.

She became putty in his hands, aware of nothing but of the sweet ecstasy that was coursing through her body. He no longer had to keep her pinned against him. Her hands were stroking through the thick scrub of his hair as she pressed against him, wildly returning his kiss, as his hands continued their onslaught. Neither felt the clothing which was the only barrier from complete intimacy.

Finally he broke away from her, but kept her still in the circle of his arms. Her eyes flew open, cloudy from passion, and she blinked several times, the way one does when suddenly awakened from a deep sleep.

'You're beautiful, Jennifer,' he said, gently touching her cheek. 'After the meeting I'll take you home with me and make proper love to you.'

Sanity returned with a rush, and she backed away from him, deliberately swiping at her mouth. 'You'll do no such thing!' she gasped. 'Do ... do you think, because you've kissed me, that you've *branded* me?'

He seemed surprised by her refusal, and shrugged. 'I thought I'd be doing both of us a favour.'

Jennifer stared at him, hardly believing her ears. 'A *favour*?' she squeaked. 'My God, what do you think I am? A woman who goes around seeking favours from a man? And who the hell do you think *you* are? The man women beg favours from?'

Andrew chuckled, the sound coming from deep within his throat. 'I have been begged before,' he admitted, and there was no mistaking the wicked gleam in his eye. 'Shall I wait for you to beg, or should I just take what I know both of us want?'

His arrogance, not to mention his conceit, amazed her. 'I heard you were in the manufacturing business,' she quipped, 'but I didn't realise you were in the stud business as well!'

'It would seem I can do most anything,' he bit back, taking a step towards her, 'except make love to you!'

'So it would seem,' she agreed, backing hastily away from him.

His arm lashed out and she felt hard fingers digging cruelly into her wrist. 'When I first saw you sitting in my father's office, I vowed I would have you.'

That was four years ago! Was it possible Andrew had entertained thoughts of her, just as she had of him? Up till now, she had tried to wrench her wrist from his grasp. Now she stopped, staring at him in surprise. Andrew sensed the change in her and slackened his grip, triumph flaring in his eyes. Unfortunately, Jennifer caught the look.

'If that were true,' she said shortly, 'I'm surprised you waited all this time to make your vow come true.'

He released her arm, tiredness creeping into his voice: 'You were obviously very much a virgin, then,' he said. 'Too young, too vulnerable, not exactly my cup of tea.'

Shocked, she could only stare at him, green eyes locked to black. Finally she managed to say, 'You've given me four years in which to grow up, is that it? Four years to lose my virginity, serve my apprenticeship, become experienced in the art of lovemaking, so that ... so that when you got me in your bed, no time would be wasted on teaching me the fundamentals?' Then, to her horror, tears sprang to her eyes and rolled down her cheeks. Helplessly, she wiped at them, but more kept coming. Andrew stepped forward and wiped them away, his thumbs a caress against her hot cheeks. When she was finally able to look up at him, she was frightened by the hardness in his eyes.

From outside, they could hear the other staff heads making their way down the corridor. Hastily Jennifer ran her fingers through her hair, straightening it as best she could. She grabbed her files and placed them where her seat was at the table and then sat down, her head bowed over her work, as Andrew opened the door for the others.

He conducted the meeting with quiet authority, moving swiftly over details which weren't important, concentrating solely on matters that were. Jennifer was amazed by his calmness, his ability to pretend nothing had happened between them. For herself, she was completely shattered, and apart from the brief report which was expected from her, she neither spoke nor smiled throughout the whole meeting. Mercifully, everyone was far too occupied with the business at hand to take notice of her, or to question her quietness.

When Andrew finally brought the meeting to an end at six o'clock, Jennifer was the first to leave the boardroom. Andrew called out to her, explaining for the benefit of the others that there was something further he wished to discuss with her, and she reluctantly waited by the door. A few minutes later he joined her, speaking in low tones so Matt, who was still seated at the table, couldn't hear.

'Are you all right?' he asked, his eyes probing her face.

'Of course. Why wouldn't I be?' She held out one little hand and had the satisfaction of seeing a concerned frown settle on his face as he viewed the dark bruise on her wrist, which he had put there. He took her hand in his and gently rubbed the discoloration, then brought her hand to his lips, kissing it tenderly. Then he had to spoil it by saying:

'Let that be a lesson to you, sweet, sweet Jennifer. I'm not a man who likes provocation!'

'Arrogant swine!' she snapped, snatching her hand from him.

His eyes glittered with amusement. 'Have dinner with me tonight,' he offered. 'I'll only be a few minutes longer and then I'll take you somewhere quiet where you can call me names without fear of interruption!'

It gave her enormous satisfaction to inform him: 'I already have a dinner date for this evening, thank you. It's with my boy-friend, a gentleman who knows how to treat a lady.'

'Is that how you like to be treated?' he returned. 'As a lady . . . or as the warmblooded woman you so obviously are?'

Her cheeks reddened to a deep crimson. 'That, my dear fellow, is something you will *never* find out. Goodnight!'

As she turned on her heel to go, he said, 'Break your date!'

She swung back to him. 'You must be mad, thinking you can order me about!'

His eyes narrowed dangerously and a ribbon of fear clutched her heart. 'Break it,' he said again.

He wouldn't dare use force against her, she thought wildly. Not with Matt still sitting in the boardroom, only metres away. Just as she was thinking this, they could hear Matt suddenly cough. The sound gave her courage. 'Go jump in the lake!' she snapped back, catching the look of surprise that she dared speak to him in such a way, before she darted down the corridor to her office.

Jennifer was grateful that the lateness of the hour meant Cheryle had packed up and gone home. She had the privacy she needed to get herself together before she met Kevin. Sitting at her desk, she held her head in her hands, fingers pressed against throbbing temples. She wondered how much more she could endure before the thief was caught and business brought back to normal. Weeks of uncertainty, plus all the overtime, was taking its toll . . . and now there was the old man's son on top of everything else.

Jennifer's cheeks burned with shame at the way she had responded to his lovemaking. Incredibly, she could still feel his hands on her body, and in a way it was true what she had said to him about being branded. He *had* left his mark on her! An indelible mark which could never be erased, for his lovemaking had not only been physical but had captured every sense her body possessed, every nerve that had, till now, lain dormant. It was as though he had taken her very soul and made it his!

Finally she got up and crossed over to her cupboard. Taking out her make-up bag, she did what she could to make herself presentable for her date with Kevin. Minutes later, she was in the lift taking her down to ground level. Outside it was raining. It was only two blocks to where she was to have dinner with Kevin, but the distance was enough to ensure she would be thoroughly drenched by the time she got there. Her eyes searched the almost deserted street for a taxi. When, after a few minutes, none came, she took the lift back up to her office to fetch her umbrella.

As she opened the door to her office, a feeling of uneasiness crept over her. Something wasn't right. Instead of entering her office, she stepped back into the reception area, her eyes scanning the layout. Then she saw what it was. Matt's door to his office was opened slightly, and she was sure it was closed when she had left only minutes earlier.

She stared at the door. Even if Matt had returned during the short time she had been away, he would never have left his door unlocked at night. It would be an unthinkable breach of security.

She walked slowly over to the door and then, taking a deep breath, swung it open. Outside in the corridor, she heard the sound of the lift, and as familiar as the noise was, it gave her a start. Then, gathering herself together, she stepped into Matt's office. She didn't turn on the light; she didn't need to. The light drifting in from the reception area was all that was needed to show Matt's safe was standing wide open. In that safe, Jennifer knew, were the latest sketches of their next campaign.

Hardly daring to breathe, she crossed over to the safe. Kneeling in front of it, she searched for the strongbox containing the sketches. It was still there, but the lid was open. She took the sketches from the box to see if they had been tampered with. Everything appeared to be in order. Jennifer was about to return the sketches to the box, when the room was suddenly flooded with light.

Reeling with fright, she swung round, expecting the thief had returned, then relief flooded over her in waves when she saw Andrew and Matt framed in the doorway. They were staring at her, Matt's face registering shocked disbelief, Andrew's face black with disgusted anger.

Slowly, Jennifer rose to her feet, the sketches still in her hand. *My God!* she thought, nausea forming in the pit of her stomach. *They think I'm the thief?* The sketches fell from her frozen fingers as though they were suddenly too hot to hold.

CHAPTER THREE

ANDREW leapt at Jennifer with all the ferocity of a jungle cat. 'You stupid little bitch!' he snarled, before grabbing her shoulders and shaking her violently. His eyes were blacker than ever she had seen them and she knew that, at that moment, he would dearly have loved to kill her.

He kept shaking her. It seemed the devil had possessed him, robbing him of all control. Her head snapped back and forth like a rag doll's, her fair hair flying as though tossed by a violent wind. Still he shook her. When he finally released her, she sank to her knees, the room whirling about her, and she was terrified she was going to be sick.

Matt helped her to stand, then guided her to the nearest chair. Gratefully she sank into it, parting her tangled hair from her face, her eyes searching for Andrew. He was standing next to the safe, staring as though in a trance, at the sketches on the floor. Jennifer saw him bend, pick them up, then toss them on to Matt's desk. He turned and looked at Jennifer, and she was further shocked by the paleness of his skin, the white line circling tight lips. She sighed and turned away. There would be no convincing him she was innocent.

Matt was fussing over her like a mother hen with an injured chick. 'Leave her be,' snapped Andrew. 'She doesn't deserve your concern!'

'Take it easy, Andrew,' said Matt, a worried frown wrinkling his brow. 'You shouldn't have shaken her like that—she's trembling like a leaf!'

Andrew laughed, and the sound was far from pleasant. 'Of course she's *trembling*! Wouldn't you, if you were caught pilfering from the office safe?'

Matt was rubbing Jennifer's hands, his eyes searching her face. 'There's got to be an explanation,' he returned. 'Jennifer is no thief.'

Jennifer's head moved automatically from one to the other as each man spoke. They were discussing her as though she was no longer in the room. Helplessly, she turned towards Andrew, her eyes sweeping up to his face. 'Matt's right, Andrew,' she declared, her voice sounding foreign to her ears. 'I'm not a thief.'

Her eyes were more grey than green, and with her hair splashed about her face, she looked extremely young and vulnerable. She shook her head. 'I'm not!' she said once again and her eyes pleaded with him to believe her.

There was no mercy in Andrew's glittering black glare and for a brief instant she even thought her denial had angered him further. She watched him square the broad width of his shoulders and his hands clench into fists at his sides. 'I don't believe you!' he replied in a coldly clinical voice.

Matt rose from where he was kneeling in front of Jennifer. 'Let it go for tonight, Andrew,' he suggested. 'We're all tired . . . it's been a long day.'

The sound of Matt's voice startled Jennifer; she had almost forgotten he was kneeling beside her. Now she turned her attention to him and was

struck by how old he suddenly looked. She
marvelled how she had never really noticed this
before. He looked old, very old and completely
exhausted. Her heart went out to him and she
reached for his hand. Matt was her boss and she
was fond of him. She was also conditioned to
obeying him—when she knew him to be right!
'Yes, Matt,' she agreed as he helped her to her
feet. 'It's late and we're tired. Let's go home.'

Matt looked hopefully towards Andrew. 'All
right with you, mate?' he asked.

Andrew smiled, slow and easy. 'Yes, you go,
Matt. We'll talk again on Monday . . . before that
if it's necessary.'

He allowed Jennifer to walk with Matt towards
the door, and waited until she had passed through
it before he ordered her back. 'I didn't give you
permission to leave, Miss Sloane. Get back here
immediately!'

Jennifer stiffened and paused, but she didn't
turn around. Her heart beat crazily in her chest.
She could feel Andrew's eyes boring into her back
and she wondered if this was how a person felt
when they knew they would be shot from behind!
Matt had paused when she had, and she sensed his
uncertainty. Poor Matt, she thought. He's torn
between leaving me alone with that *monster* and
his loyalty to Andrew, who was, after all, the old
man's son. She tucked her arm in his, a gesture she
had done so many times, and smiled up at him.
'Come on, Matt,' she said, surprising even him
with the calmness in which she spoke. 'He can't
keep me here against my will.'

'Oh, yes, he can!' a sugary-sweet voice purred from behind, and Jennifer and Matt turned as one and stared at Andrew. He was lounging in the doorway, leaning lazily against the frame, legs crossed at the ankles. When he had come into Matt's office, he had had his jacket on. Now, they saw, he had removed it and his shirt sleeves were rolled halfway up his deeply tanned arms. Like he's prepared to do battle once more, Jennifer found herself thinking. Her eyes strayed from the fine black hairs that worked in a vee down to his wrists, up to his face, black eyes mocking them with devilish amusement.

'You go, Matt.' Andrew repeated his earlier invitation, and Jennifer's heart seemed to thud its way to her throat. Matt would leave now, she knew. There was no mistaking the underlying current of authority in Andrew's voice. Her arm fell from Matt's and she caught the gleam of triumph that flared briefly in Andrew's eyes as he watched the gesture. It was obvious to her then that he wanted his pound of flesh and was determined to get it.

'It's all right, Matt,' she told him softly, knowing full well that he still hated to leave her behind, but that there was really nothing he could do about it. 'I can handle myself, so there's nothing to worry about. Go home, as Andrew says, and get some rest. I'll be fine, really.'

She watched Matt go, and it wasn't until she heard the whirring sound of the lift outside in the corridor that she turned to face Andrew. 'That was very rude of you,' she accused him. 'Matt doesn't deserve that kind of treatment!' Her eyes had restored themselves to their usual deep green and now they flashed angrily in Andrew's direction.

The corners of Andrew's mouth curved into a lazy smile. 'I wasn't rude to Matt,' he said. 'I merely allowed him a chance to escape, which was what he wanted.' The smile deepened as he crooked a finger at her. 'Come, Jennifer,' he said, his voice soft but at the same time very deep, 'let's return to the scene of the crime, shall we?'

She shrugged a dainty shoulder and lifted a hand to tuck her hair behind her ears. Her earlier fears were behind her now. After all, she *was* innocent, and no amount of interrogation would prove otherwise. Andrew would be left with egg on his face and forced to apologise to her. A smile tugged at the corners of her mouth as she imagined herself refusing to accept it.

Andrew caught the faint smile and watched her thoughtfully as she swept past him to take the chair she had vacated earlier. He followed her into Matt's office and went to the cupboard which was similar to the one in her own office. 'Matt used to keep some brandy ... ah, here it is,' he said, extracting a bottle from the cupboard. He got two glasses from the same shelf and poured them each a drink. Jennifer refused to accept the glass he offered her. 'No, thank you,' she said, smiling sweetly. 'I don't need false courage to face up to you!'

His eyes narrowed dangerously and she felt the smile leave her face. 'Take it!' he barked, and she reached out for the glass, her fingers trembling slightly as she held it. 'Drink it,' he ordered, and she brought the glass to her lips and drank. Immediately she felt the burning sensation in her throat as the amber liquid made its way to her stomach, warming her and settling her nerves. Andrew took the glass from her, his strong brown hand circling hers, and she snatched her hand away, painfully aware of the tingling sensation that coursed up her arm from his touch. There was a wicked gleam in his eyes as though he knew how his merest touch affected her. Jennifer turned her face away in an effort to protect herself from the potency of those devilish black eyes, warning herself that she must be very careful if she was to come out ahead during the interrogation that was sure to follow.

Andrew carried her glass plus his own drink to Matt's desk. He put her glass down and held his own cupped in his hand as he sat on one corner of Matt's desk, long legs stretched in front of him, silently viewing her. The calming influence of the brandy quickly left her as he pinned her down under the fierce intensity of those deadly black eyes. She felt a nervous knot forming in the pit of her stomach and took a deep breath in an attempt to unravel it.

The breath she took was more like a gasp, oddly pathetic in its sound. Andrew's eyes became softer, almost sympathetic, and his voice was gentle when he quietly asked her, 'Why were you in such a rush to leave the meeting tonight?'

The question, and the manner in which it was

asked, confused her. She had expected a hard line
of questioning, fired at her in rapid succession. She
wouldn't even have been surprised if Andrew had
placed a naked light bulb in front of her face! But
his question was natural enough, delivered in a
friendly conversational tone. Automatically, she
felt herself relax.

'I . . . I . . . well, the meeting was over, wasn't it?'
she asked him, traces of her earlier confusion
lingering still in the soft green of her eyes.

He smiled and her heart flipped crazily in her
chest. 'Yes, the meeting was over,' he agreed, the
same gentleness still in his voice. 'But why did you
feel it was necessary to be the first one out of the
door?'

'I don't think I was the *first* one,' she answered
carefully, thinking there must be some importance
to the question. 'Bill was the first out of the door,'
she suddenly remembered, her eyes shining
triumphantly.

'Only because he's bigger than you,' grinned
Andrew, teeth flashing white against the dark hue
of his skin. 'I watched you wrestle with him for
first place.'

She raised a slender hand to her mouth to
suppress a laugh, but some of the sound came
through. 'Did I?' she asked on a chuckle,
remembering now that she had.

'Yes . . . you did,' he confirmed, his smile
deepening. 'I was terrified you might hurt him!'

Her chuckles grew in volume until she was
laughing openly, the laughter sparkling in her eyes
and a soft pink staining her cheeks. Bill easily

weighed two hundred pounds! The idea of her hurting him was hilarious. 'I wonder if he checked himself for bruises when he got home?' she gasped, still laughing.

Andrew finished the last of his brandy and placed his glass beside the one she had used. 'You still haven't told me why you were in such a hurry to leave,' he reminded her of his question.

Jennifer stopped laughing. How could she tell him it had been torture to sit through the meeting after what he had done to her? Even now, the memory of his hands exploring her body and the way in which she had so eagerly responded filled her with shame. She had needed to escape from the thrillingly sensuousness of the man, but that of course was something he must never know.

'Was it because you were anxious to meet your date?' he asked, providing her with the excuse she needed.

'Yes,' she answered, relief flooding her eyes. 'I was afraid I'd be late.'

He pushed himself away from the desk and walked over to the safe which was still open. 'And yet,' he said, watching her carefully, 'you were still here forty-five minutes later!'

Jennifer's eyes widened in horror and her jaw fell open. It came to her too late that Andrew had deliberately set out to trap her, and she had fallen for it hook, line and sinker. He had skilfully manoeuvred her until she had been caught in her own lie. How could she ever hope to prove her innocence now? she wondered dismally, as the sick feeling she had experienced earlier, returned to the pit of her stomach.

'Well, I left . . . but I came back.'

'Why?'

'It was raining. I came back for my umbrella.'

'At the very most,' he said, 'it would take you ten minutes to go downstairs and back up again. What did you do for the remainder of the time?'

'I didn't go downstairs right away,' she mumbled, feeling as awkward as a ten-year-old child caught raiding the cookie jaw.

'No?' a question.

'No,' the answer.

He sighed his impatience. 'Well, are you going to tell me what you did do before you went down, or are we going to spend the evening playing guessing games?'

'After the meeting . . . I came to my office.'

'To work?'

No, not to work! she wanted to scream. *I came back to my office because you'd upset me! I'd never been kissed like that before and I felt confused! My head was spinning and I felt as though you'd turned my world upside down!*

'Yes, to work,' she answered miserably, tiredness creeping into her voice.

'Do you usually work in the dark?' he asked softly.

'Of course not. . . .' Her voice trailed off as once again she realised too late she had been caught in another trap.

Andrew chuckled, the sound coming from deep within his throat. 'That's right, my sweet, sweet

Jennifer! Matt and I walked past here not ten minutes after you left the boardroom. Had you been in your office, we would surely have seen light shining from the shaft. As it was, we didn't, and even with your beautiful cat's eyes, I doubt you could see sufficiently to work in almost total darkness!'

'Well, I wasn't actually working,' she answered in a small voice.

'No? What were you doing then . . . actually?'

'I . . . I was thinking . . . about the thief.'

'Were you?' His voice was clipped. She knew he didn't believe her.

'Yes—yes, I was. I often sit in the dark . . . and think.'

'About thieves?'

Her eyes swept up to him and a deep flush crept over her cheeks. 'No . . . usually about other things. But tonight . . . tonight I was.' She nibbled on her bottom lip and her eyes were wide and very green as she watched him. She rushed on, aware of how weak her story must sound, but determined to tell him everything . . . almost . . . in order to avoid being caught in any more skilfully laid traps. 'I sat at my desk for a while, I don't know for how long, just thinking, as I've told you. I finally got up, combed my hair and then took the lift down to the ground floor. It was raining, so, as I've said, I came back to get my umbrella.'

She paused before continuing, realising she hadn't had a chance to tell him what had happened next. She leaned back in her chair and shut her eyes trying to remember every little detail.

When she opened them again she was startled to see Andrew watching her, a harsh look of contempt in his eyes.

'Thinking in the dark again?' His voice was openly sneering.

Helplessly, she nodded, turning her head away to avoid the contempt in his eyes. 'It's a habit I've had since childhood,' she told him. 'Whenever I'm trying to remember something important, I first shut my eyes and then try to recreate the scene.'

He came over and stood in front of her. 'And you're trying to remember something important now?' he asked, and she ignored the sarcasm in his voice.

'Yes,' she sighed. 'When I walked into the reception area, I got this strange feeling. I remember it made me feel uneasy ... a little scared.' She gazed appealingly up at him, to meet his coldly cynical glance. Her eyes dropped from his face and she continued in a small voice, 'I walked over to the door of my office when something struck me. At first I wasn't sure what it was, but then I noticed Matt's door was open and I was sure ... no, positive ... that it had been closed when I left earlier.'

'Then what?' he prodded her memory, watching her closely, fierce black eyes raking her face. She shifted uncomfortably in her chair, knowing how he must be enjoying watching her squirm. She squared her shoulders and continued bravely:

'I pushed Matt's door open ...'

'You said it *was* open!' he reminded her harshly.

'Well, it was,' she floundered, pink staining her

cheeks. 'I pushed it open *further*, was what I was going to say before you so rudely interrupted me!' she glared up at him. 'At first I didn't see it. Everything appeared to be in order.'

He bent forward, placing his hands on either side of her chair causing her to lean back, away from his disturbing closeness. Her eyes swept up to meet his as though drawn there by a magnet and she felt her heartbeat quicken.

'See what?' he asked, a cruel smile curving his mouth. 'Are you going to tell me Matt's window was open as well and that a carrier pigeon had the sketches in his beak, but that you managed to grab them from him just before he flew out the open window?'

'Of course not!' she snapped, her green eyes flashing angrily. 'I saw that the safe was open. I didn't notice immediately because the room was in shadow.'

He straightened and walked over to the desk, his hands stuffed into his pockets as he stared down at the sketches. 'Bloody things!' he snarled, one hand snaking from his pocket to scatter the sketches wildly about Matt's desk. He swung round on her and she shrank from the black anger in his face.

'Were the sketches still in their box?' he lashed out.

'Yes,' she answered quickly. 'I ... I was so relieved. Nothing had been touched.'

'Then what were they doing in your hands?'

She blinked in confusion, spreading her hands helplessly. 'I took them out to check them, to make certain they were all right. That's what I was doing when you and Matt came in and frightened me half to death!'

He let out his breath in a long drawn out sigh. 'If you didn't open that safe, then who did?'

'I don't know, but I swear it wasn't me.' She caught the look of scornful disbelief on his face. 'Please, Andrew, you've got to believe me,' she pleaded desperately.

His eyes narrowed thoughtfully as he leaned against the desk and the look he gave her was deliberately mocking.

'I've found out enough for one night,' he told her.

'Does that mean you believe me?' she asked hopefully.

His smile matched his eyes for coldness. 'No, it means it's getting late and I don't want to keep you from your dinner date with your boy-friend!'

Relief that she had been let off so easily swept over her in waves. 'You mean I can go?' she asked gratefully, then looked at her watch. 'Kevin must be wondering where I am—I was supposed to meet him at seven.'

'Kevin—so that's his name. Kevin who?'

'Kevin Livingston,' Jennifer supplied, uneasiness creeping over her at the dangerous glint in Andrew's eyes. 'I . . . I've been dating him on and off for quite some time now,' she added without knowing why, while he watched her, his eyes probing her face.

'On and off?' and she watched, fascinated, as one black brow rose in a majestic arch. 'It couldn't be very serious between the two of you if it's an "on-again-off-again" romance.'

'Oh, I don't know,' she shrugged, 'perhaps it just means neither of us has met anyone we like better.'

'Like?' He walked over to her chair and pulled her from it, his hands circling her wrists in a vicelike grip. '"Like" is a strange word to use for a man who must be your lover!'

He released her wrists and she could have moved away had she wished, but the strong sexuality that rose between them held her there, rendering it impossible for her to move. It was an invisible bondage from which she had no hope of escape. She licked lips that had suddenly gone dry and looked up at him, helpless against the thrust of his sheer male potency.

'He's ... he's not my lover,' she managed, but she couldn't hear her own voice above the roaring, throbbing beat at her temples.

Andrew smiled at her and the smile matched the cruelty in his eyes. He reached out a long tapering finger and caressed her cheek. She shuddered against his touch and his smile deepened. 'Have you *ever* had a lover?' he asked softly, his hand cupping the side of her face.

'No,' she shook her head.

'But you want one, don't you.' He was stating a fact, not asking a question, and he bent his head to kiss her. She responded eagerly, moving closer to him, practically begging him to take her in his arms. She clung to his lips as a drowning person would cling to a lifeline, but still his arms remained loosely by his sides. Her nostrils quivered at the sweet male scent of him and her lips danced to his tune. Each tiny ember that had ever sparked within her was brought to a roaring inferno as his mouth sought out every tastebud, lingering only long enough to remind her of her famine!

She found her fingers in his hair, tunnelling through the thickness, tracing the outline of his head. Her body was pressed against his in a way which later she knew would shame her, but right now it was obeying instincts that she was powerless to resist.

His mouth broke from hers in a cruel detachment that swept through her body. Shock waves rippled through her blood stream, shattering each highly strung nerve. She felt him reach behind his head to disentangle her fingers from his hair. It was the only time his arms had been around her.

She gaped up at him, her green eyes wide and her lips sore and swollen, still parted from his kiss. He ran a finger lightly across them, but his smile did nothing to hide the glint of anger that sparked in his eyes. 'I've warmed you for Kevin,' he rasped. 'Now I'll take you to him.'

What he was implying shook her out of her reverie. Stunned and deeply hurt by his words, she could only think of one action. With a cry of outrage, she lifted her hand to lash out at him. But he had anticipated her action and caught her hand in a deadly grip. 'It's only fair to warn you,' he snarled between clenched teeth, 'that had you struck me, you would have received the same back!'

'I see,' she gasped, hating him with the same intensity that she had loved him only minutes before. 'An eye for an eye, is that it?'

'Exactly!' he bit out, dropping her hand.

She watched in disbelief as he crossed the room to take his jacket from the peg on which it hung and calmly put it on. He was totally heartless, she decided, completely without regard for anyone's feelings. He was deliberately ignoring her, and she decided to do the same. She went to the desk and began gathering and sorting the sketches, humming softly as she placed them in their proper sequence. After laying them carefully in their box, she knelt by the safe, aware all the while that Andrew was watching her.

Still humming, she placed the box in the safe and then locked it.

'Who has the combination to the safe?' asked Andrew, as she stood up.

'Just Matt and I,' she answered casually, still feigning indifference to his presence.

'How often is the combination changed?' he asked.

'Once every fortnight. We're given the new combination on a card and destroy the card after we've committed it to memory.'

He drew in a ragged breath. 'So no one ever has access to the combination other than you and Matt?' he enquired.

Jennifer shook her head. 'No one!' she declared emphatically, proud of their security.

'Matt was with me, so he couldn't have been stealing the sketches from the safe. That leaves only one other person who could have possibly opened that safe.'

'What . . . what are you implying?' she gasped.

He smiled, a slow lingering smile. 'You had me fooled,' he drawled, 'but I must admit your act was very convincing. You don't look like a thief, but then thieves seldom do.'

'Just what are you *saying*?' she begged again, anguish flooding her eyes.

'I'm saying the obvious,' he answered slowly, his eyes raking her face in disgust, 'and the obvious is . . . you're guilty. Guilty as hell!'

CHAPTER FOUR

'THEN why don't you call the police and have me arrested?' Jennifer challenged him directly, hands on hips. 'Better still, I'll save you the trouble and ring them myself,' she flared, grabbing the phone from Matt's desk, her hands shaking with frustration and anger.

Andrew wrenched the telephone from her grip and shoved the instrument across Matt's desk well out of her reach. 'When the time comes,' he assured her coldly, 'I'll drive you to the police station myself. In the meantime, I intend finding out what turned a beautiful young lady to a life of crime.'

'Finding out?' she snapped. 'What's that supposed to mean? That you'll be spying on me?'

He shrugged his broad shoulders. 'Unless you have something to hide you shouldn't really care.'

'I care because I don't have something to hide, can't you see that?' she asked earnestly. 'My God, I'm not a criminal, and I refuse to be treated as one!'

'It was your hand holding those sketches,' he reminded her coldly.

'Yes, but it wasn't me who unlocked that safe!'

'Well, it sure as hell wasn't Matt, and you're the only two who have combinations to the safe. And if I remember correctly, you were the only one at the meeting who was unwilling to accept that the thief could be one of the staff. You preferred to think it might be an outsider.'

'Yes, and I still do,' she answered firmly.

He grabbed her by the shoulders, his fingers digging cruelly into her flesh. 'Come off it, Jennifer,' he snarled. 'You've already told me only you and Matt have the combination. Now you're saying someone walked in off the street and opened that safe, as if my magic. Either come up with a better theory or admit your guilt.'

She shook her head helplessly. She knew the situation looked bad for her, but there was nothing she could do to change it. 'I can't come up with a better theory,' she finally admitted. 'But I'm not going to confess to something I haven't done either.'

His hands dropped from her shoulders. 'Get your things,' he ordered her impatiently. 'I'll drive you home. There's no point thinking your boyfriend will still be waiting for you.'

She shot him a scathing glance before replying. 'Kevin will be waiting for me,' she said. 'I've been later than this and he's still been there.' She reached up a slender hand to carelessly flick back her blonde hair, hoping she appeared untroubled and nonchalant in the face of her accuser. She couldn't think of anything worse than having to sit beside him while he drove her all the way home. Thank God she had this date with Kevin, a legitimate excuse for not accepting his offer, and having to listen to him accusing her, demanding the confession he was certain she owed.

She stood stiffly next to him on the way down in the lift. Outside on the street he guided her to his car, a late model sleek grey Jaguar. After settling her in the passenger seat, he took his place behind the steering wheel.

'Where to?' he asked drily, the first words either had spoken since leaving Matt's office.

'The Spinning Top Disco,' Jennifer answered. 'It's not far from here, only a couple of blocks down Castlereagh Str . . .'

'I know the place,' he snapped, cutting in on her directions while he turned the key in the ignition. The motor zoomed to life and they sped out into the street. Jennifer clutched at her seat, terrified that at any moment they would crash, but soon relaxed when she saw the easy manner in which he manoeuvred the car through the traffic.

The earlier lull in traffic was now over, with the usual Friday evening merrymakers out in full force.

Within minutes Andrew drew up beside the Disco, bringing the car to an abrupt halt. Small groups had formed outside the doors and there was a constant stream of gaily dressed people going in and out the large swinging doors. Music blared on to the street. Andrew turned to Jennifer and she saw the distaste on his face, so she wasn't in the least surprised when he said, 'The Spinning Top Disco is nothing short of a dive. I'm amazed that you should like a place like this.'

She didn't like it, but she wasn't going to give him the satisfaction of admitting it. She shrugged instead and said, 'Why should it amaze you? I should think it would be exactly the kind of place you would think I would like. Kevin and I love this place,' she continued matter-of-factly. 'We come here every chance we get. All our friends hang out here and you always end up meeting some very interesting people.'

She looked across at his stony features, guessing that for himself, Andrew would probably prefer death to being caught at the Spinning Top. The pompous so-and-so! It gave her pleasure in thinking.

'What kinds of people?' he asked sarcastically. 'Dope addicts, pimps, drop-outs ... people like that?'

'Yes, people like that,' she quipped, her green eyes flashing impudently, and she couldn't resist the opportunity to goad, 'And once I arrive there will also be a thief!'

A hand snaked out to grab her wrist and she gasped as his fingers bit into her flesh. 'Don't push me, Jennifer,' he warned, his eyes glittering with anger. 'I could easily take your smart-alec remarks as a confession, you know.'

'You don't frighten me,' she lashed back, amazing even herself with her bravery. 'You'd just love to think you caught the thief right off the bat, wouldn't you? To have accomplished in a single day what we weren't able to do over a period of several weeks. Well, you're barking up the wrong tree, mister, and the sooner you realise it the sooner you might get around to catching the *real* thief!' She wrenched her wrist from his grip. 'And when you do catch the real thief I shall expect an apology from you for the manner in which you've so shabbily treated me.'

'You're forgetting,' he ground out, 'that as far as I'm concerned I have caught the real thief!'

Her breath caught in her throat and tears of exasperation stung her eyes. 'Yes, how could I forget that?' she answered bitterly. 'It's not enough that you've accused me wrongly, you want to torture me as well!'

A cruel smile matched the look in his eyes. 'The idea of torture hadn't entered my mind, but now that you've suggested it,' he taunted, his eyes raking the fragile beauty of her face, 'I must say the idea has merit!'

A shiver raced up her spine and she backed closer towards the door. 'You're a fiend!' she whispered, her voice trembling so as to make speech difficult. 'A devil!'

His eyes lingered on her mouth and she licked her lips nervously, her hand reaching for the handle of the door as she frantically tried to open it. Andrew surprised her by reaching across to open it, swinging the door wide and thereby providing her with her means of escape. She made no effort to get out, his nearness unsettling her more, she suddenly realised, than his accusations had! She looked up at him, her eyes wide with confusion.

'Well?' He raised an inquisitive brow. 'This is your favourite place, remember? All your interesting friends are waiting eagerly, I'm sure, to greet you. Kevin must have his fingernails chewed to the quick wondering what's happened to you.'

Her cheeks flooded with colour at his smugly arrogant remarks. 'Yes, of course,' she answered quickly, stepping hastily from the car and away from his snide comments. She stood with her hand on the door looking at him, wondering why she just didn't turn and dart into the disco. His eyes held hers and her heart leapt at the dangerous flare that ignited their depths. Then he turned away from her, twisting the key in the ignition, and she was certain that had she not stepped back when she did, he would have run over her.

She watched the car until it rounded a corner and was lost from sight. Miserably she turned and went into the disco searching the crowd for Kevin. She spotted him almost immediately, his fair head towering over most of the other dancers on the floor. When the dance ended and he was making his way back to his table she beckoned to him by waving her arm. He came immediately to where she was standing, a welcoming smile lighting up his boyish features.

'I was beginning to think you weren't going to make it,' he said. 'They've stopped serving dinners.'

'It's all right,' she told him. I won't be staying, Kevin. I've had a long hard day and I think I'll just grab a cab and go home.'

'You're sure?' he asked doubtfully. 'You won't stay for even one drink?'

'No, I'm tired, and I think this music is a little too loud for me tonight.' She smiled up at him, thinking how nice it was to look into a pair of blue eyes which held no threat, totally unlike Andrew's eyes, so fiercely black and penetrating!

But when she finally got home and into bed, it was only to spend a sleepless night wondering and worrying what was to become of her. It seemed fate had struck her a cruel blow, sending Andrew back into her life just to have him brand her a thief. She wondered if it was possible to love somebody and hate them at the same time. For love him she did, and her cheeks burned at the memory of his hands and his mouth exploring her body. But she also hated him—hated him because he had been so quick to believe the worst of her, proof enough that what she felt for him, he obviously didn't feel for her.

Self-pity swept over her and she relished it, treating it like a soothing balm for her poor troubled heart. When she finally slept it was to dream she was in jail and that Andrew was her jailer. It was a relief when morning finally came. She got up and stood on her balcony.

Below was the harbour with its small fishing and sailing craft on the sparkling clear waters. The stretch of golden beach was washed clean from the outgoing tides and except for one or two joggers was completely deserted. The famous old Manly pine trees swayed in the soft sea breezes while the fronds of palm trees hummed their own special tune. The sun hung like a gigantic yellow beach ball against the brilliance of a royal blue sky. The colours were so vibrant that they reminded her of the drawings she used to do when she was a child, with the sky, the sun and the water all painted in unnaturally bright colours. Yet here they all were.

Jennifer turned from the scene below to get

dressed. But instead of putting on a pair of jeans and a T-shirt, her usual gear for Saturday morning clean-up, she slipped into a bright red bikini. Minutes later she was racing along the sand, pausing only long enough to drop her towel and beach robe in an untidy heap, before plunging into the cool green water.

She was an expert swimmer, having been taught by her father who had coached at the local swimming club when she was a child. By the time she was five, she had mastered every stroke, and before many years had passed after that, her bedroom had been filled with trophies. Now she swam out into the water, cutting through the surface in clean even strokes. As she swam, she felt the tensions easing from her body, and by the time she returned to her pile on the beach, she was totally relaxed. Last night's nightmares and her fears seemed ludicrous in the face of such a God-given, glorious day.

Drying herself with the fluffy white towel she had brought from her unit and then, shrugging into her beach robe, she decided she would go for a brief jog before returning home to her chores. She jogged for a quarter of an hour and then perched on some rocks at the far end of the beach to watch a luxury liner pass through the heads on its way to its mooring. The huge, gleaming white boat barely seemed to move as it inched its way through the water carrying its passengers from distant lands to holiday for a short while in the sunny warmth of Sydney's beaches, before sailing off again to explore yet another land.

Jennifer shaded her eyes with her hand, watching the liner until it rounded the heads and was lost from her view. With a sigh she got up from the rocks and walked slowly back down the beach and to home. When she arrived at her unit, the door was open and the sound of soft music drifted out to greet her. Cautiously, she tiptoed down the short hall leading to the lounge room. No one was there, but a record was playing on her stereo and a folded newspaper lay on a chair beside it. She cocked an ear and listened. From the direction of the kitchen she could hear someone moving around and *whistling*! No one she knew whistled—at least, she had never heard anyone she knew whistle.

It was morning and as she had left the door opened the way she had found it, she felt reasonably secure as she tiptoed her way to the kitchen. After all, if need be, she could always scream for help. Besides, the milkman was making his rounds outside in the corridor. As she approached the kitchen, the whistling stopped and a deep baritone voice boomed out in flat accompaniment to the record now playing on her stereo.

Her trespasser was standing with his back towards her, waving an egg lifter in one hand, while he rocked a frying pan over the grill of her stove. A tea-towel was wrapped around his waist and tied in a knot at the back. A light beige cashmere sweater ruffled the jet black hair at his neck and his sleeves were rolled almost to his elbows, revealing the tanned skin of well-muscled forearms. Chocolate brown slacks outlined the lean hardness of his thighs.

The table was set for two, she saw, and she noticed also that he had used her best tablecloth, her finest crystal, her never-used-before Wedgwood dinner set and her silver cutlery willed to her by her grandparents. A single long-stemmed yellow rose, which he must have brought himself, stood in a slender vase and had pride of place on the table.

Jennifer leaned against the frame on the doorway, a grin spreading slowly across her face as she watched Andrew prepare their breakfast. So, she thought smugly. Obviously his presence meant he had come to apologise. Perhaps Matt had convinced him that she wasn't the thief. Well, she sure wasn't going to make things easy for him, but at the same time she decided she had better be on her toes. As he turned she quickly replaced her grin with a frown and tightened the sash of her beach robe.

'Enjoy your swim?' he asked casually, as though this was what he generally asked her each morning while he fixed breakfast.

'Yes, the water was great,' she replied just as casually.

'And your jog?' he asked, as he flipped eggs on to plates.

'The jog, too,' she agreed, thinking he must have been watching her every movement on the beach.

'Didn't that ocean liner look magnificent passing through the heads? I had a great view of it from your balcony,' he added conversationally as he placed bacon on their plates.

If he had come to apologise he was certainly taking his time about it, Jennifer decided ruefully as he passed by her to get two glasses of freshly squeezed orange juice from the fridge. 'I watched it from the far end of the beach,' she told him.

'Yes, from the rocks. You looked rather lonely sitting there by yourself.' He smiled, kicking the door of the fridge shut with his foot while she watched disapprovingly the rough treatment her little fridge was receiving. 'Do you often walk along the beach?' he enquired casually as he carried the juice to the table and set it by their plates.

So he *had* been watching her. She might have guessed. 'Every chance I get,' she admitted, wondering just what it was he was up to. 'How did you get in here?' she demanded.

'The janitor let me in,' he explained easily. 'I told him I was a friend, and he didn't argue.'

Who would? she wondered. Andrew was the sort of man one would avoid arguing with! 'Well, what are you doing here, then?'

'You mean apart from cooking breakfast?' he asked innocently.

Jennifer sighed her impatience. 'Yes. Apart from using my best china, my best everything, just what are you doing here?'

He held out a chair, deliberately avoiding her question. 'If you will be seated, I shall bring on the toast.'

It would hve been both churlish and childish to refuse to sit at her own table and eat her own food, so after a slight hesitation, Jennifer found herself accepting the chair he was holding out for her. She picked up the neatly pressed napkin by her plate. 'My best Irish linen napkins!' she moaned. 'Do you realise I'm a working girl? I don't have the time to fuss over linen. Besides, they're only for special occasions.'

'But how special can an occasion get?' he countered, taking his place across from her and beaming broadly. 'It's a beautiful morning, the sun came up on yet another day and we both have our health, wealth and happiness.'

What was he getting at? wondered Jennifer as she viewed him through narrowed eyes. She picked up her fork and took a few nibbles. 'I have *one* of those three things you mentioned,' she said. 'I doubt many people, apart from yourself of course, would have all *three*.'

She was being deliberately sarcastic, but after yesterday, she was determined to keep one step ahead of him.

Her sarcasm didn't disturb him in the least, she saw, as he calmly spread her butter on her toast, before putting it in his mouth. The nerve! she fumed inwardly.

'Yes, I suppose I have all three,' he agreed between mouthfuls. 'Mmm, this is good, isn't it? I always fry eggs in butter. None of that dripping for me,' he confided as though sharing the chef's secret of the year with her. The coffee had finished percolating, so he got up and poured them each a cup, asking her if she took cream and sugar, and when she answered yes to both, he spooned in the sugar and tipped in the cream. Jennifer winced at the sound of the silver coffee spoon tapping at the sides of the Wedgwood cup as he briskly stirred her coffee.

'I never take cream and sugar in my coffee,' he stated, in that same conversational tone which was beginning to drive her quite mad. 'Too much sugar isn't good for you—and of course there's all that cholesterol in cream.' His smile was benevolent as he sat back down again, pressing her lovely linen napkin to his lips. It was bad enough to watch him stuffing himself with her food, without having to watch him wiping his mouth on her linen. She had been hoping he wouldn't use it and she had no intention of using the one beside her plate, pushing it well out of reach of any grease splatters that might touch its snowy fabric.

'Well, Jennifer,' he said, pushing himself away from the table with his coffee cup in his hand, 'you haven't told me which of the three states you're lucky enough to have.'

'What do you mean?' she enquired, watching the careless manner in which he held the cup.

'Health, wealth and happiness,' he reminded her of their earlier conversation.

'Oh, that,' she said, sipping carefully from her cup, hoping he hadn't chipped or cracked it when he had stirred her coffee. 'I have health,' she answered smoothly. 'Until yesterday, I also had happiness. Wealth?' she shrugged her dainty shoulders. 'Wealth has always avoided me.' She gazed across at him, green eyes sparkling. 'Does that answer your question?' Her smile was sugar-coated.

Andrew returned her smile and she watched him closely. 'Happiness can be a swim in the surf, a jog on the beach, an ocean liner chugging through the heads, can't it?' he asked softly, black eyes mocking her.

'Yes,' she answered also softly, matching his tone, 'but up until yesterday, happiness was a job I enjoyed, with people I liked.'

His eyes gleamed across at her. 'The job is still there, and so are the people.'

She laughed. 'But the happiness is gone,' she said, 'and that's what we're discussing, isn't it? Happiness?'

Andrew watched her over the rim of his cup, an unreadable expression in his eyes. Was it sadness? she wondered, and then decided it couldn't possibly be. Andrew would never be sad for anyone in his life, let alone sad for her and her unfortunate situation.

'How . . . how did you find out where I lived?' she asked, more to change their topic of conversation than for any other reason; although now that she had asked the question, she was curious as to how he had come by her address.

He studied the coffee in his cup. 'I checked the personnel records,' he admitted, not a trace of guile in his voice.

'Did you go to work this morning?' she asked. 'You must be an incredibly early riser!'

'As a matter of fact, I never work on a Saturday if it can be avoided.' He drained the last of the coffee from the cup and poured himself some more, not bothering to ask Jennifer if she wanted another. 'I found out yesterday where you lived. When Dad asked me to take over for a few weeks I asked him if he still had you at the agency. When he said you were still there, one of the first things I did was to check your files.'

'What a typically arrogant thing for you to do!' she bit out, detesting his smugness. 'Personnel records are highly confidential—you had no right to snoop into my personal history!'

'I wasn't snooping, as you so quaintly put it, I was merely seeking an address. Once I had your address, I closed your file and put it away.'

'I just bet you did! My address was probably the *last* thing you read, after you'd first found out every little detail of my life!' She stood up from the table, her voice trembled with fury. 'You could have asked Matt for my address ... you could have asked me. Had I wanted you to have it, I would have given it to you. Had I wanted to invite you to my home, I would have done so. Had I wanted to invite you for breakfast, God forbid, I would have done that as well. But you had to just grab, didn't you? You had to sneak behind my back and then force your way into my home, using all my things and cooking up all my food. Then ... then you *spied* on me down at the beach, watching my every movement. What for?' she rasped, unable to control herself. 'Did you think I would be having a rendezvous with a fellow thief? Did ... did you go through all my personal belongings searching for names and contacts?' She slammed her small fists on the table top, not hearing the rattle of her Wedgwood and silver as the table shook. Tears of indignation, frustration and hurt rolled unchecked down her cheeks. 'Come on, Andrew, tell me,' she pleaded, 'what exactly did you expect to find? That I was running a syndicate for organised crime?'

Throughout her outrage Andrew had remained calm, watching her with the same amount of amusement he would have watched a live show. Now he stood up and leaned across the table, his black eyes only inches from her green ones. 'I looked up your address because I wanted to know where you lived, because I fully intended dating you. Last night, after I dropped you off at the disco, I cursed myself for allowing you to go into that joint. This morning when I woke up, I was still cursing myself, so I decided to come over and see how you were.' He straightened up and glowered down at her. 'I arrived in time to see you shallow-diving into the waves. It struck me that you probably hadn't had breakfast and that you'd be hungry after your swim. The janitor is a reasonable man and . . .' he shrugged, stuffing his hands in his pockets.

'I don't believe you,' Jennifer said softly. 'I believe the main reason, possibly the only reason, you came here was to spy on me. Last night you accused me openly of being a thief. To quote you, you stated quite firmly that I was as guilty as hell. Well, you've put me through hell, all right, and I don't trust you as far as I could throw you. You had no right to enter my apartment without my consent or knowledge. You had no right using my best china and my cutlery and for *breakfast*, of all meals!' She tapped her fingers on the tablecloth and then picked up one of the napkins. 'I should make you pay for the laundering of these,' she said dismally, before putting the napkin down.

He picked up the napkin she had just discarded, examining the make embroidered on one corner. 'They're very nice,' he acknowledged, tossing the one he had held alongside the other on the table. 'And this dinner set,' he said, picking up his coffee cup. 'Wedgwood, isn't it?'

'Yes,' she breathed, 'please be careful with it. The set cost a fortune.'

'I can imagine,' he acknowledged, banging it down on the table top and picking up a silver spoon which he turned over in his hand. 'Sterling silver,' he read aloud. 'Heavy, too!'

'Give me that!' she cried, grabbing the precious spoon of her grandmother's from his hand.

'You have some very nice things in your possession,' he mocked her, a devilish gleam in his eye. 'And an extremely expensive harbourside apartment to keep them in. For a single lady with a fairly modest income you live extremely well!' His eyes raked her face sneeringly, while she gaped up at him her eyes filled with dread by what she saw in his face. 'It makes one wonder how one manages it, wouldn't you agree?' he added caustically before taking his leave.

Jennifer remained by the kitchen table where he had left her, staring down at the expensive piece of silver still in her hand.

'My God!' she whispered hoarsely, dropping the spoon on to the table.

CHAPTER FIVE

JENNIFER's nightmares continued. She slept through them by night and lived with them by day. Her possessions haunted her. The gleaming silver cutlery mocked her, as did the Wedgwood dinner set. She no longer enjoyed the view from her balcony.

She was convinced that Andrew had come to her home to check her possessions, to see what a thief would buy with stolen money, she thought over and over again. Never mind that she had been collecting her dinner set since she was a girl of fourteen, with money earned from baby-sitting jobs and jobs during school vacations. Never mind that the cutlery had belonged to her grandparents and willed to her. Never mind that she had been collecting junk furniture for years and restoring the various pieces which now furnished her flat, or that she had bought the crystal cheaply at an auction sale. Never mind that it had taken her years of hard work to have what she now owned. And as for her unit . . . her father had cashed in an insurance policy which he had taken out for her when she was a mere baby and she had used this as a deposit on the unit. Her father had done the same for her sister and her brother. But as usual, Andrew had jumped to conclusions, not giving her the time nor the opportunity to explain. Now it made her appear guilty, because Jennifer knew not many girls would have in their possession what she had. She realised as she looked around her flat that an outsider might even consider her wealthy, or that she had suddenly come into a fortune!

Saturday merged into Sunday, and Jennifer wondered if Andrew had discussed his suspicions with his father. Had he seen Matt? Had they held a private meeting to discuss her fate? Would Andrew call a special board meeting and, in front of everyone, point the finger of guilt at her? Would she still have a job?

When Monday morning finally came, Jennifer dressed carefully for work. She chose a light grey business suit, its severity lessened by a white ruffled-neck blouse. Her make-up was applied sparingly and she drew her blonde hair back behind her ears, kept in place by little black combs. As she viewed the results in the mirror, she was pleased. She looked like an efficient, no-nonsense business lady. She certainly did not look like a thief!

Her anxieties increased as the hydrofoil brought her closer to work, and when she waited at the intersection to cross the street, she could see the agency directly in front of her. What if everyone at work already had been told she was the prime suspect? She felt the warm rush of blood flood her cheeks. How terribly embarrassing it would be to walk past them, knowing they would be whispering about her.

The doorman greeted her in his usual manner, as did the mail clerks and anyone else she ran into on her way up to her office. If Andrew had condemned her, it would only have taken minutes for the news to get around that the thief had been caught redhanded, and that she was the thief.

When Jennifer entered the reception area, Andrew was standing in front of Cheryle's desk. Cheryle was obviously pleased to be the centre of Andrew's attention, Jennifer saw, as the girl blushed prettily while thanking Andrew for complimenting her on her new perfume. 'You don't think it's too strong, do you?' she asked him, holding out her wrist for him to sniff. Andrew took her wrist and sniffed appreciatively, and Jennifer watched in disgust.

The flirt! she thought. Any girl would be helpless against Andrew's persuasive charms, she knew, and she wouldn't have been in the least surprised if Andrew knew as well—the fiend! How she detested him!

Jennifer closed the door behind her and the sound caused Andrew to turn around, Cheryle's wrist still in his hand. 'Ah, Jennifer,' he said, 'you're late.' He sniffed at Cheryle's wrist once more. 'Beautiful,' he told the girl. 'Definitely not too strong.' He patted her hand and gave it back to her, and Jennifer thought she would be sick.

He swung his attention back to Jennifer. 'Five minutes late,' he drawled. 'I was beginning to wonder if you'd decided not to come in today.'

'Were you?' she enquired stiffly, going up to Cheryle's desk and deliberately ignoring him by her side. 'Have you sorted the mail, Cheryle?' she asked.

'Yes, Miss Sloane,' answered Cheryle. 'I've opened it and placed it on your desk.'

'Thank you, Cheryle.' The perfume was definitely too strong, Jennifer thought as she passed Cheryle's desk to her own office. Kevin had given her some like it a year or so ago, and she had found the scent overpowering and had ended up dumping it down the sink. But she had never forgotten the smell.

In order to dissuade Andrew from following her into her office, in case it was his intention to do so, Jennifer paused before opening her door. 'See that I'm not disturbed, Cheryle,' she said pointedly, still ignoring Andrew. 'I'll be busy until my first appointment at ten.'

'Very well, Miss Sloane,' replied Cheryle. 'What about telephone calls? Shall I take messages, or pass them through to you?'

Jennifer hesitated. She didn't want to give Andrew the impression she passed too many responsibilities on to Cheryle, but telephone calls could be a real nuisance, especially when she had so much work to do. 'Pass only the ones you can't handle yourself, Cheryle.'

'Mr Livingston rang earlier. He said he'd ring back at nine-thirty. Should I put him through?'

Jennifer shot a look at Andrew. Had he remembered Kevin's name was Livingston? she wondered. It was obvious from his slightly sardonic scowl that he had. She smiled.

'Yes, of course, Cheryle,' she answered. 'You know I always take Kevin's calls!'

If Cheryle was surprised at this fabrication of

fact, it didn't show on her face, Jennifer was relieved to see.

As Jennifer sat at her desk, she was aware that her hands were trembling. So he was still spying on her, she thought glumly, checking to see what time she arrived at work and chastising her in front of Cheryle for being five minutes late. How dared he, when she had put in countless hours of overtime without added pay!

The door burst open and Andrew sauntered in with an armful of files.

'What are you doing here?' she demanded breathlessly, startled by his unexpected appearance. 'You heard me tell Cheryle I was busy and didn't want any intrusions.'

'Of course I heard, but naturally I assumed you couldn't possibly mean *me*,' he smiled benevolently, spreading his files across her desk.

'What do you think you're doing?' she gasped, as the space on her desk slowly disappeared.

He grabbed a chair and sat opposite her, opening one of the files. 'Working!'

'Working? Here? At my desk? In my office?'

'Yup!' And she watched in incredulous disbelief as he rolled up his sleeves and bent his dark head over the file. 'You wouldn't happen to have an extra pen, would you?' he glanced up, smiling at her startled appearance. 'I didn't think to bring one.'

She opened her desk drawer and selected a pen. Passing it to him, she looked at him in unconcealed disgust and in no mood to mince words. 'You've come to *spy* on me, haven't you?'

'For lack of a better word, I guess you could call it that,' he agreed easily, flicking the pages of the file.

'Why, you ... you despicable, pompous, overbearing brute!' she lashed out, tears of frustration and anger springing to her eyes. 'How do you expect me to work under these conditions?'

His glance encompassed the room, taking in the smartly appointed furnishings, the air-conditioning unit, the stereophonic speakers recessed in the walls. 'Oh, I don't know,' he drawled. 'Everything seems very nice to me.'

'You know what I mean!' she hissed, a dark flush staining her cheeks. 'How can I concentrate with you breathing down my neck?'

'I'm sure you'll manage.' His dark glance revealed his thoughts; she had managed to steal, she could manage this.

'Well, I can't, and I refuse to be intimidated. I'm not guilty and I have nothing to hide, and I refuse to be treated as if I might! Either you have me arrested for suspected theft or leave me alone. You might be enjoying this little game you're so intent on playing, but I'm not.'

Andrew's brows drew together in a black frown, his eyes glittering with anger. He seemed about to say something, then obviously thought against it as he bent his head over his files. 'Shut up!' he snarled. 'Get to work!'

Fussing and fuming inwardly, Jennifer grabbed her own files and spread them before her, taking as much room as possible and receiving a great deal of satisfaction when Andrew was forced to relinquish some of his space. The Corser Car Products had top priority, but with Andrew sitting across from her she found it next to impossible to concentrate. It angered her that her own presence didn't seem to disturb him at all. In fact, the speed with which he was going through his files made her wonder if he had forgotten he was supposed to be spying on her! She nudged one of her own files close to the one he was working on, moving it until it eventually slid over what he was reading. He looked up annoyed and she smiled in satisfaction.

'Oops!' she murmured. 'Sorry, but I'm not used to sharing my desk.' She glanced at her watch. 'It's almost ten o'clock,' she reminded him.

'Forget about your coffee break. You haven't done enough work to warrant it.'

She glared across at him. 'I wasn't referring to a coffee break. I have an appointment at ten and if you don't mind I'd like to clear my desk.'

'All right,' he surprised her by agreeing, and she watched while he gathered up his work. 'Well?' he growled when she made no move to do the same. 'Now that you've seen how it's done I suggest you follow suit.'

Arrogant swine! thought Jennifer, as she quickly closed her folders and put them away. Thank God he would be leaving when her client came in. But when Cheryle ushered in Mr Cullens, Andrew made no move to go. Jennifer watched horrified as he merely settled himself in a chair next to Mr Cullens, his mocking smile daring her to object. Her green eyes blazed with anger, but somehow she managed to introduce the two men and proceed with the meeting. Several times she caught Andrew's glances of approval, and despite his unwelcome presence she was proud of how well the meeting was going and that he could see for himself what a clever business lady she was.

While Mr Cullen's head was bent over the contract she had managed to win for the Agency, Jennifer shot Andrew a triumphant smile as the contract was signed. Andrew escorted Mr Cullen to the lift, and while he was gone, Jennifer flopped into her chair sighing with relief. Now maybe Andrew would believe that anyone who worked so hard for their firm couldn't possibly turn around and steal from it. Feeling enormously pleased with herself, she was surprised when she saw it was almost one o'clock. The meeting with her client had gone on for almost three hours. The phone beside her rang and picking it up, Jennifer smiled when she recognised Kevin's voice. While she was speaking to him, Andrew returned, and she frowned when he took his place at the desk, making no attempt to disguise the fact that he was listening to her conversation.

'Excuse me, Kevin,' she said into the mouthpiece, 'someone's listening.' Putting her hand across the mouthpiece, she glanced scathingly at Andrew. 'Do you mind?' she hissed. 'This is a private call.'

'Really? Well, I suggest you cut it short. I'm taking you for lunch.'

'Sorry, but I already have an invitation for lunch.'

'With Kevin?' he smirked.

'Yes, if you must know.'

'Not today, you aren't. Today you'll lunch with me.'

'Like hell, I will! I'd rather starve than eat with you!'

She saw the way his face became taut, a deep flush spreading across the hard angles of his cheeks. She didn't see his hand snake out and grab the phone, slamming it down on its cradle with a ferocity that terrified her. She backed away, alarm clearly visible in the oval pallor of her face. He caught her by the arm and dragged her to him, the rugged dark planes of his face remorseless and determined. 'I warned you not to provoke me,' he muttered, staring at her mouth, and she gasped as his face swooped down at her.

He hurt her, and she knew he did it deliberately; his kiss violent and cruel as he crushed her lips until she lost all feeling in them. His hand was around her throat, forcing her to keep still, and she felt like a tethered animal under the cruel hands of her master. When at last he released her, she felt the taste of blood in her mouth. 'You beast! You hurt me,' she whispered angrily, swiping at her mouth.

'I wanted to hurt you,' he ground out. 'You're forgetting you're on borrowed time here and while you are, you'll do as I say. Now get your bag. We're going for lunch and you can tell that boyfriend of yours that he's not to ring you during office hours.'

His flashpoint anger frightened her, terrified

her, but still she couldn't resist saying, albeit a trifle timidly. 'I'll go, but I won't eat.'

'You'll eat!' And she shivered knowing she wouldn't dare not to.

They drove to a quiet seafood restuarant on the quay overlooking the harbour and from where they sat they could see the magnificent Sydney Opera House, its slender lines in the shape of sails. Andrew ordered seafood salads for them both and Jennifer found she did, after all, have quite a healthy appetite, eating everything on her plate down to the last scallop.

'That was delicious!' she declared, and he half smiled at her, causing her to look away in confusion. She had been aware of the change in Andrew's attitude towards her ever since they had left the agency. It was as if he had decided to call a truce during their lunch hour and she was determined she wouldn't say or do anything that might upset him. He was really quite charming, she decided, when he chose to behave like a human being instead of an animal. Her gaze took in his dark good looks and she sighed wistfully, wishing things had turned out differently.

'Something wrong?' he asked. 'You seem rather pensive.'

'I . . . I was just thinking about Matt,' she lied. 'I haven't seen him all morning.'

'I've given him a few days off. He came in looking rather bedraggled this morning, so I sent him home.'

'Oh?' That meant she didn't have Matt to protect her against Andrew. No one to intervene.

No one in her corner. 'He's not sick, I hope?' she asked anxiously.

His smile was barbed. 'No, more in a state of shock.' He peered at her over the brim of his wine glass. 'Matt still thinks you're not our thief.'

She swept her eyes up to meet his. 'I'm not,' she said simply, and as she looked into his eyes, she knew that more than anything else in the world, she wanted him to believe that. But his eyes were without expression as he changed the subject.

'That outfit you're wearing is in sharp contrast to the dress you had on last Friday. Trying to change your image?'

Jennifer flushed, her hand reaching up automatically to touch the white collar circling her neck. Was she so transparent that he could guess at everything she did? 'I ... I often wear this,' she answered, avoiding his eyes. 'It's very practical.'

'I like it.'

'You do?'

'Yes, it gives you an air of efficiency. You handled Cullens well. You're good at your job,' he stated matter-of-factly.

Jennifer's mouth fell open at the unexpected praise and she decided to quit while she was ahead. 'I'd better get back,' she murmured. 'We only take an hour for lunch.'

'Relax—you're with the old man's son.' Jennifer stared at him and he laughed softly. 'Sure, I know everyone calls Dad "the old man". He knows it too. We laugh over it. He's the old man ... I'm the old man's son.' He tipped up his wine glass and mocked a salute. 'Here's to us both.'

Jennifer couldn't be sure if Andrew was being sarcastic or if he resented his father's staff calling his dad the old man. Probably Andrew himself resented always being referred to as the old man's son. He caught her frown and guessed the reason behind it.

'Don't worry your pretty little head over nicknames,' he told her.

'How is your father, Andrew? We rarely hear anything about him, except the odd thing Matt tells us.'

She saw the far-off look that came into his eyes and caught the sadness that hovered briefly across his face, before he smiled, completely masking his true feelings.

'For a man his age, he's in great shape,' he said. 'If you would like, I'll take you to visit him, say, next Saturday afternoon.'

Her green eyes sparkled at the unexpected invitation. She would dearly love to see the old man again, and Saturday afternoon would be perfect. But then the light began to fade from her eyes. What if Andrew was inviting her for the sole purpose of exposing her in front of his father? She knew Andrew could be cruel, but could he be so cruel as to deliberately humiliate her in front of a sick old man. She gazed across at him and the last of the sparkle disappeared completely from her eyes, leaving instead a sick kind of dread.

'I—I don't know,' she faltered, toying with her water glass. 'I might be busy. It's too early in the week to plan so far ahead.'

'You mean, of course, that Kevin hasn't asked

you out yet and you feel you should keep the day open for him.' It wasn't a question, it was a statement, and she shuddered under the coldly cynical glint in his eyes.

'No!' It was a sharp retort and Andrew raised his brows in an arrogant gesture.

'No?' he queried. 'Just "no"?'

'I'm not waiting for Kevin to ask me out. I might have to work.'

'No one works on Saturdays,' he challenged.

'We've been working Saturdays. The campaigns . . .' Jennifer lowered her eyes and nibbled on her bottom lip. 'Then there's always work at home. You know,' she attempted a lighthearted laugh, but somehow it got lost in her throat, 'the scrubbing and the cleaning, the shopping and the ironing.'

The waitress came to enquire if they wanted dessert. 'Not for me, thanks,' she told Andrew, so he ordered himself peach melba and coffees for them both.

'I should be getting back,' she said once more as she sipped at her coffee.

'Relax,' he told her. 'You're with me. What can anyone say?' He gave her a smile which was highly suggestive, and her heart skipped crazily in her chest. They both knew gossip would be rampant if they arrived late from lunch together. She couldn't meet the challenge in his eyes and she turned away, the shining fall of her hair outlining the slender column of her neck. 'You haven't told me,' he said, 'how your date with Kevin went the other night.'

Back to Kevin again. 'It was all right,' she answered on a sigh.

His black brows rose majestically. 'Just "all right"? Not magnificent? Not fantastic? Didn't you meet any of those *interesting* people you said you always meet at the disco?'

She glared across at him. 'I had a headache—which wasn't surprising, considering what you put me through before I got there!'

He seemed to like that. A smile slid slowly across his face. 'Pity!' he murmured, and she would dearly have loved to wipe that smug look from his face. 'I trust Kevin was sympathetic and took you home early?'

'As a matter of fact, I took myself home early.'

'Oh? But you didn't have a car,' he frowned.

'That's right,' Jennifer replied lightly. 'There was no point in spoiling Kevin's fun, so I grabbed a cab.'

The frown deepened. 'Good of Kevin to look after you so well. Sounds like a great boy-friend—but then I guess a lady can't expect much from an off-again, on-again romance.'

'Guess not,' she quipped, with a great show of nonchalance. She had scored a point, she decided, and she smiled brightly to prove it.

Andrew's eyes narrowed slightly as he studied her. 'What does Kevin do?' he asked.

'You mean work?'

A mocking smile slanted the strong line of his mouth. 'Yes, I mean work. He does work, doesn't he?'

'Yes, of course he does. As a matter of fact,

Kevin used to work at the Agency, but now he's in business for himself . . .'

'He used to work at the Agency?' Andrew interrupted to ask. 'I can't remember anyone by that name working for Dad.'

'Kevin started after I did. You would have been in Europe, Jennifer explained.

'How long did he work there?'

'Not for very long. A year, I think.'

'Which department?'

She laughed. 'You seem terribly interested in Kevin!' A teasing smile danced along her lips. 'Perhaps you should give me the name of one of your girl-friends, so I can have fun quizzing you about her.'

His black eyes mocked her. 'You'd hate hearing about the ladies in my life, so let's just keep on the subject of Kevin, shall we? Which department did he work in?'

Her green eyes flashed angrily. 'There's no need to talk to me in such a harsh manner!' she flared. 'And for your information, I *would* hate hearing about your girl-friends. I couldn't imagine a more boring subject,' she huffed.

'Nor could I,' he agreed with a smile. 'But for the moment, I'm rather interested in discussing one of your boy-friends—which you seem very reluctant to do.'

'Reluctant?' she queried. 'I'm not at all reluctant to discuss Kevin, in fact I rather enjoy it.'

His black eyes narrowed dangerously as he glowered at her. 'Sales!' He growled the single word.

'What?' she blurted, a puzzled frown creasing the smooth line of her brow.

'Sales!' Andrew repeated grimly. 'Kevin would have been in Sales at the Agency.'

'You've won the jackpot,' Jennifer attempted to laugh, but somehow it never made it past her lips. 'But what made you guess?'

He shook his head, dismissing her question. 'And I'll wager he's still in sales, but in a different line.'

Jennifer's eyes widened in astonishment. 'Right again. Kevin is in real estate.'

Andrew leaned back in his chair and dragged his hand through the thick scrub of his hair. Suddenly he looked very tired, dark shadows crossing his eyes. 'It puzzled me,' he began slowly, 'how you could manage the caper all on your own, but now everything has slipped smoothly into place.'

The muscles in her stomach tightened. 'Wh-what caper?' she asked weakly, knowing full well what he meant.

'Oh, come now, Jennifer,' he answered harshly, 'stop playing the innocent.' He reached out and grabbed her wrist, pulling her close to him. 'The campaigns which have been stolen!' he ground out. He dropped her hand and she stared down at it. Two red marks appeared, in sorry contrast to her pale skin. She dragged it across the table and let it fall on to her lap.

'Stop it!' Her voice came out in a shudder. Their luncheon had been going so well, why did he have to spoil it by accusing Kevin and bringing up the thefts? How much more did he think she could stand? 'Stop it!' she said again, shaking her head from side to side. 'You don't know what you're talking about.'

'Don't I?' he lashed out. 'Then suppose you enlighten me.'

Jennifer couldn't speak. Her cheeks were pale and her eyes had grown dark with misery. His eyes glittered with anger as he watched her.

'The fact Kevin worked at the Agency means he would know all our procedures,' he answered for her. 'Being in the sales department he'd know which organisations would jump at the chance to get hold of a Thorpe ad. Ads which you, my little sweet, steal for him!'

Jennifer passed one trembling hand through her hair, knocking out one of the little black combs. Her fine blonde hair tumbled against the side of her cheek, and absently she flicked it back, tucking the wispy strands behind her ear. Her eyes never left Andrew's face.

'What you're saying,' she whispered, and he had to lean forward to hear her faint remarks, 'what you're saying just isn't true, and Kevin would be as shocked as I am now if he knew what you've accused him of.'

'Not half as shocked as he's going to be when I confront him with it,' he jeered.

'You wouldn't dare!' she gasped. 'My God, but you're mad! Kevin is no fool, let me warn you. He'd take out a slander action against you!'

Andrew gave a cynical smile. 'I doubt he would be capable of any direct action. Any man who'd hide behind a woman's skirts while she steals for him, probably has cotton wool for a backbone.' He reached across and picked up the little black comb which was still on the table where it had fallen. He turned the comb over in his hand, studying the small object as carefully as if it were a priceless jewel, and smiled as he handed it back to her. 'Very pretty,' he said.

Jennifer snatched it from his hand. 'It wasn't expensive, if that's what you were thinking,' she flared, sticking the comb back into place. 'I only paid a dollar for these combs.'

His smile deepened as he watched her tuck it into her hair. 'Well, after all, you didn't get the campaign Friday night, so you had nothing to sell over the weekend. You and Kevin will have to do some budgeting now, mm?'

Jennifer grabbed her bag, at the same time pushing herself away from the table. 'I think this lunch has gone on long enough,' she said, starting to rise from her chair. 'I can't remember a time where I've spent a more detestable hour, and I can only hope that you've enjoyed my company even less than I've enjoyed yours!'

Andrew was on his feet and helping her from her chair, a deep-throated chuckle sounding wickedly cruel as he helped her to her feet. With his hand on the small of her back and his darkly sensual mouth only inches from hers, Jennifer found herself helpless against the strangely potent power he seemed to wield over her. His hand moved lightly up her back and she felt herself trembling under his touch and her cheeks grew hot as she saw in his eyes that he was perfectly aware of the effect he was having on her. She could feel the chair at the backs of her legs and told herself the chair was preventing her from moving back and away from his touch. Andrew's smile became even darker as he guessed at her dilemma. His hand moved back down her spine and she fought against the sensations that trickled through every nerve of her body. Suddenly he released her, smiling as he reached into his breast pocket to remove his wallet, holding her eyes with his own as he drew out two notes and tossed them on the table without a glance.

'Ready?' he asked, and she nodded, not trusting herself to speak with lips that had gone suddenly dry. As he led her from the restaurant, she was grateful for the darkened interior which masked her discomfiture from the other patrons. Outside in the brilliant sunshine he placed his hands on her shoulders. Her eyes swept up to meet his and she willed herself to gaze at him squarely and not shy away like some frightened, skittish little animal. He searched her face, going from the high cheekbones to the pert little nose, down to her mouth which was trembling slightly and then up to her eyes. Her eyes held his attention. They were a curious mixture of an innocence which had suddenly . . . perhaps too suddenly . . . been forced to awaken, and in the clear green pools he saw that she was afraid. His grip tightened on her shoulders and his voice when he spoke was gentle, the same gentleness he had displayed before and which she found far more disarming than any of his deliberate acts of cruelty.

'You haven't given me your answer about Saturday,' he reminded her now. 'I'll be busy myself in the morning, so would two o'clock suit you?'

Jennifer's gaze faltered and she could no longer meet his look. Her eyes dropped from his and when they did she felt as if she had been released from a hypnotic trance. How like him, she thought now, to browbeat her all through lunch and to accuse her and Kevin of being partners in such a devious crime. It was obvious from his persistence that he was determined to see her destroyed—and yet he had the audacity to casually remind her of his offer to take her to visit with his father. Of course she wouldn't go. How could she, when it could only mean that the noose around her neck would only tightened?

'Yes,' she heard herself agreeing, 'two o'clock would be just fine!'

CHAPTER SIX

LATER that same afternoon, Jennifer sat alone in her office trying to shut Andrew from her mind and concentrate on the work at hand. As soon as they had arrived back from lunch Andrew had been called to settle a problem with a video display, but she knew that as soon as the problem was sorted out he would be back in her office.

She sighed and pushed her work away. Why had Andrew suddenly decided to accuse Kevin as being her accomplice? If she was the thief then perhaps she might have involved Kevin, but seeing that she wasn't it was ridiculously absurd to even think of such a thing. It worried her terribly to think Andrew might confront Kevin with his wild accusations. Kevin was a good friend and she didn't want him hurt on account of her.

She finally managed to dictate some letters for Cheryle and carried the tape out to give to her at her desk. Cheryle wasn't there, so Jennifer left the tape where she would be sure to see it, and as she turned to go back to her office, the telephone in Matt's office rang. She went in to answer it, but then hesitated when she saw it was Matt's special 'hot line' phone ringing. Only Matt's special clients had the number, and always the calls were of paramount importance and for Matt's ears alone. When the phone continued ringing she decided to answer it and tell the caller Matt was at his home and could be contacted there. A series of sharp claps rattled into her ear and then a voice hissed across the wire some sort of message which Jennifer found hard to decipher, but it sounded like some sort of warning—'Stay away from there', or something to that effect.

Then the line went dead and she knew the caller had hung up. Puzzled, she stared at the phone still in her hand and then, frowning, placed it on its receiver. Obviously a crossed wire somewhere, or perhaps some child playing a trick. She thought nothing more of it and decided to get the Corser Car Products campaign from Matt's safe. With Matt away a firm decision had to be made concerning its fate.

Back in her own office she spread the campaign in front of her, jotting down fresh ideas and changes as they occurred to her. Reaching up, she plucked the two little combs from her hair and held them in her hands the way Andrew had, and a wistful smile appeared on her lips. If only there was some way she could prove to him that she was innocent, then how happy she would be. Sighing heavily, she placed the two combs in the drawer of her desk, then shrugged out of her suit jacket to resume work again on the Corser display. While she worked she half expected Andrew to return—and then she realised she was hoping, actually hoping, he would.

Finally, her work with the campaign was finished; now it would be up to the Art Department to bring it to life. Gathering the files, she stepped out to the reception area. Cheryle was once more at her desk, the telephone to her ear. When she saw Jennifer she started guiltily and then quickly put the receiver down. Jennifer smiled. Obviously Andrew had warned Cheryle against too many personal phone calls as well!

'I'm going down to the Art Department, Cheryle, if anyone needs me,' she said, noticing as she passed Cheryle's desk the bottle of perfume there. It was exactly the same bottle Kevin had given her. She picked it up and sniffed it. God, it was awful! How could Cheryle, never mind Andrew, possibly like it? She put it back on Cheryle's desk and shuddered when Cheryle picked it up and dabbed more of the revolting stuff on her wrists and behind her ears. 'Kevin gave me some of that once,' Jennifer said on impulse. 'Did you buy that yourself, or did someone give it to you?' she asked, almost sympathetically.

Was she imagining it, or was Cheryle deliberately avoiding her eyes? The girl grabbed a piece of paper and rolled it into her typewriter. 'It was a gift from a friend,' she mumbled as she bent her head to correct the paper line.

Jennifer watched her, wild, insane thoughts whirling in her head. Could Kevin have given Cheryle that perfume? she wondered. Was Cheryle the inside contact while Kevin worked the outside? Was Cheryle the thief?

'Cheryle, where were you earlier?' she asked casually.

'I was at Printing until an hour ago. Why, is something wrong, Miss Sloane?'

'I . . . I received a rather muffled telephone call

earlier. It came through on Matt's special line.'

'I didn't put it through, Miss Sloane. As I've said, I was at Printing, but I did instruct the switchboard to hold any calls. I'm sorry you were disturbed.'

'No, that's all right, Cheryle. It's just that it puzzled me at the time. I couldn't really make out what the caller said, but I guess it wasn't important.'

My God, thought Jennifer as she took the lift to the Art Department. What am I doing, pointing my finger at poor Cheryle and suspecting her and Kevin of espionage? How could she be so cowardly as to try to shift the blame from herself to two innocent people? To treat a mere coincidence of both her and Cheryle having the same perfume into something sinister was nothing short of scandalous. Her cheeks burned with shame. Poor Kevin, she thought. He had been a trusted and loyal friend for a long time and totally incapable of anything devious. Cheryle was an excellent secretary, reliant and trustworthy. Her only consolation lay in the knowledge that neither one would ever know what her dreadful thoughts had been.

Of course she realised why her imagination had run away with her. She was so smitten by Andrew that she was willing to toss anyone to the lions. She had been accused unfairly, but she wasn't going to do the same thing herself. During lunch she had had the distinct impression that Andrew was willing, albeit a trifle reluctantly, to give up the idea that she was the thief. It was only a feeling and she had wondered if Matt had been able to convince him of her innocence, or if her own performance with her meeting with Mr Cullens had changed his mind about her. Perhaps it had even been a combination of both, but whatever it was, he had been definitely more relaxed with her.

Even when he had sat at her desk, she was sure now he hadn't come to spy on her, that had been her suggestion, but just to tease her, perhaps to get even with her for being rude earlier.

But whatever it was, his attitude had changed dramatically when she had told him Kevin had once worked at the agency. He had said he wondered how she could have managed on her own, so perhaps it was this which had given him second thoughts, but once he knew Kevin had worked in the Sales Department, then the wheels of suspicion had begun turning again.

Jennifer stepped out of the lift. What a mess! she decided dismally. Whatever the outcome of this whole miserable affair she decided she would behave normally, carry on her duties as best as she knew how and hope that eventually everything would work its way out.

It struck her as she walked down the corridor leading to the Art Department that, despite Andrew's suspicions of her, she *trusted* him to believe in her. As incredible as that seemed to her, she knew Andrew would never go to the police unless he was absolutely one hundred per cent sure that she was guilty. She smiled ruefully, knowing he wasn't one hundred per cent certain she was innocent, either. He would be a ruthless foe, but at the same time she knew she could count on him to be a staunch friend. Friend? If only he knew how much she wanted him to be far more than that!

She opened the door to the art room thinking he must never know how she felt about him, or how deeply her feelings ran. The Art Department was her favourite area at the agency. It was bright, busy and colourful. Talent oozed from every nook and cranny and there was always the delightful odour of paints and textures. As she entered the huge area where the artists worked, her eyes rested on Andrew as though drawn there by a magnet. He looked up and saw her at the same instant. Jennifer hesitated. She hadn't known he would be here, although she realised he could be anywhere in the building.

He started towards her and she saw he had removed his suit jacket and that the cream-coloured shirt he was wearing enhanced his deep tan. His eyes swept over her and a lazy smile drifted across his handsome features. It made her aware that she had also removed her suit jacket and that the white ruffled-neck blouse and close-fitting skirt were receiving his full attention. She stiffened, selfconsciously moving her hand up to brush back her hair. The gesture reminded her that she had also removed her combs as she pushed back the smooth fall of hair resting against her cheeks.

'What brings you to the Art Department?' asked Andrew in a drawl. 'Did you know I would be here?'

His conceit was truly amazing! 'No, not really,'

she answered glibly. 'But when I was outside the door, I received some pretty nasty vibes, so I thought you might be!'

His soft laughter spread over her like a cloak of warm velvet, drawing her towards him with invisible threads. A smile tugged at the corners of her mouth and shone through her eyes as she gazed up at him, her pupils dilated with happiness because she hadn't expected to find him here, but here he was. His eyes seemed to caress her face and the smile which had been on his lips remained there and she dragged her eyes from his because she knew it must be obvious how she felt towards him and despised herself for her weakness.

A long finger reached out to hook her chin and she was forced to meet those incredibly black eyes once again. She shivered under his provocative gaze, the touch of his hand causing a warm flush to creep across her cheeks. Her own heartbeat roared in her ears and she thought he must surely hear it.

'Jennifer.' His voice was husky as he said her name and she found it impossible to avert her eyes from the smouldering black pools which had arrested them. His hand reached up to cup the side of her face and she felt, more than heard, his sharp intake of breath. 'Let's call a truce,' he suggested raggedly, his hand dropping from her face in a gesture similar to defeat.

Her heart came to an abrupt halt and then thudded spasmodically against her ribs. She clutched her files closer to her chest and swallowed hard, her eyes unnaturally bright with gratitude.

So she had been right, it hadn't been her imagination. Andrew was willing to concede that she wasn't the thief and now that he had had a chance to think about it, had obviously decided that Kevin was innocent as well. A truce wasn't a full pardon, but it was a step in the right direction. A big step.

She reached up a hand to tuck the shining fall of her hair behind one pink little ear, unaware that her hand was trembling. 'Yes, a truce,' she breathed gratefully, her voice barely a whisper.

Andrew shoved his hands into his pockets, an unreadable expression masking his eyes. 'We can't very well be feuding all the time around the staff,' he continued reasonably. 'Everyone's under enough pressure as it is.'

Jennifer glanced over her shoulder, his mention of the staff making her aware for the first time that someone could possibly be watching them, even though the entrance to the Art Department was some considerable distance from the actual working area. Everyone seemed intent on their work and her eyes shifted back to Andrew, but most of the light had disappeared from them. It was the staff he was considering, not herself. He had called a truce and he expected her to go along with the charade. Nothing had really changed. He still believed she was guilty.

She managed to control a shudder and gave him a stiff, surrendering smile. 'We shall pretend nothing has happened. We shall pretend that last Friday evening never existed. We shall pretend that I'm not a thief and that you are not my accuser.' She cast him a sideways glance. 'Have I got it right?' Her brightness was forced.

Andrew looked down at her, one hand thrust into his pants pockets, his feet slightly apart. His rugged features were sternly masculine and forbidding to the point of almost complete indifference.

'Something like that.' His response was emotionless.

Jennifer dropped her eyes to the files she was holding, blinking rapidly to hold back the tears. He reached out and took them from her, flicking through them as he carried them to one of the large display tables, and she watched as he bent his head over the sheets studying the changes she had made. She walked slowly over to stand next to him, gearing herself for the criticisms she felt sure he would make. At last he came to the final page.

'These are good,' he surprised her by saying. She hadn't realised she had been holding her breath and now she let it escape in a gesture of relief. She knew her work was excellent, but she didn't mind in the least settling for good.

'Thank you,' she heard herself saying. God, she sounded like a pre-schooler who had finally managed to put her first drawing together for the teacher to admire! 'I used the original campaign as a guide, of course, changing only the colours and the print. Actually, I think it makes the whole campaign much better. It's bolder, much brighter.' It was, in fact, what she had originally suggested for the campaign, only to have her ideas vetoed by Matt, who preferred to stick with tried and true methods of advertising. Her eyes swept up to meet his mocking gaze. 'I'm glad you like it,' she finished by saying.

'I said it was good . . . I can't remember saying I liked it!' He picked up one of the sheets. 'The lettering is far too large. It takes up too much of the label.'

'It's not too large. It's bold! There is a difference, you know,' she defended.

'And there's a difference between a label and a magazine cover!' he returned sarcastically. 'The lettering is far too large.'

She grabbed the sheet from him, her cheeks flushed and her eyes the colour of a turbulent sea. 'The Corser people are forward-looking. They appreciate originality. They won't find this lettering too large, they'll find it . . . dramatic!'

'And bold?'

'Yes,' she snapped. 'Dramatic and bold!'

'Unfortunately, they're not the ones who have to come up with a solution of how to fit the lettering on to the label.' He slanted her a slightly sardonic smile. 'The idea was good, as I've said, but it's not practical. You've just managed to waste more time.'

Jennifer gathered up the folders, her hands shaking with agitation. When she had them in a tidy heap she turned to face Andrew, and with great difficulty managed to sound quite calm. 'I would like the chance to discuss the lettering with the artists. If they say it can't be done, then I'll accept it and go back to our usual methods.'

He studied her thoughtfully for a few seconds,

then reached down to pick up one of the folders, opening it at random.

'Perhaps if you use all lower case . . . get rid of the caps, it might work. I like the idea of black on white with the product drawn in red. It's all very clearly defined.' He tossed her a crooked smile. 'All very dramatic, all very bold.' He picked up the stack of folders. 'Let's see what they can do with it,' he suggested, turning towards the senior group of artists.

Jennifer put her hand on his arm and he looked down at it, causing her to quickly withdraw it. 'Not the senior artists,' she said in answer to his darkly quizzical brow raised in a somewhat mocking slant. 'I . . . I thought I'd use the junior artists.'

'What!' The single expletive sounded like a quiet explosion to her sensitive ears, but even so she had been prepared for his reaction. Using junior artists for a campaign as big and as important as the Corser group justified more than a raised eyebrow. He was looking at her as though she was from another planet with no inkling of earthly customs. 'Junior artists!' he repeated, his tall figure erect as he stared disbelievingly down at her. 'Are you mad?'

'They deserve a chance.' Her voice was softly pleading. 'The juniors did all the preliminary work for the original Corser campaign, and it's not as if they have to start from scratch. Sizes and shapes will remain the same, only the colours and lettering have to be changed.' Again she reached out to touch his arm, but this time he did nothing to discourage the gesture. It was only when the hardness of his forearm brought the sensitive nerves of her fingertips to life, sending a tingling sensation coursing up her own arm, did she realise what she was doing. She snatched her hand away, but not before she had caught the curiously mocking smile which hovered on his handsome mouth and reached up to add even more depth to satanic eyes. 'I promise to accept full responsibility,' she finished by saying, her voice sounding as though it had been strained through a sieve.

A low, rumbling laugh came from his throat, and as Jennifer snapped her head up at the sound she had the curious sensation that she was watching a storm. His face was black, the rumbling from his throat was like thunder, and it seemed as if lightning flashed in his eyes. She took a step backwards, certain she had managed, somehow, to release the devil in him.

'You promise to accept full responsibility? How terribly generous!' he taunted, his eyes narrowed into slits as he watched her.

'Y-yes.' She took another step backwards, wishing she could turn and flee from the piercing arrows of his eyes and from the lash of his tongue which bit into her like a whip. The distance between them gave her a small amount of courage. 'That's exactly what I intend to do,' she offered in a tremulous voice.

'And how do you propose to do that ... *exactly*? Where does full responsbility end and foolishness begin ... *exactly*?' A single step removed the distance she had managed to put between them, but there was nowhere for her to go, she realised, as the corner of the table bit into her back. Andrew's eyes glared down at her. 'Even the senior artists would find it hard to wrestle with the new lettering you've proposed. How in blazes do you expect a handful of youngsters to cope?'

'I'll show them.'

'You?' His sharp bark of laughter was an insult to say the least, but it robbed her of her fear and fuelled her with a fresh fighting spirit. The fiery light in her eyes matched his for brightness and her voice was every bit as cold.

'Yes, *me*!' She squared her shoulders and met his eyes, the sweep of her lashes enhancing the clear green. 'First off ... they're not youngsters, they're artists, and damn good ones at that. They're just as bored with old ideas as I am, and they'll jump at the chance to do something excitingly new and different.' She raced on, not giving him an opportunity to interrupt. 'They will like working with the colours, and I've read that people are attracted to the colour red. Customers will buy a product with red featured on a label before they'll buy one with any other colour. The lettering is bold in its simplicity and it won't be hard for the artists to get the hang of it. A few practice squiggles to experiment ...'

'Experiment! Need I remind you that the Corser group are among our largest accounts? You don't experiment with people like them, girl, and you sure as hell don't use juniors to do it with!'

'Then who's going to do it?' she snapped. 'You?

Our head artists are flat out keeping up with all the back work. Other campaigns are waiting in the wings. We can't thrust this one on them as well and this campaign must be finished within two weeks. That's when our deadline is up.'

'Then get some more artists.'

'Oh, sure,' she scoffed. 'And where do you propose I get them? Good artists don't grow on trees, you know, and you certainly can't go down on the streets and call for them.' She slanted him a sideways glance. 'In *your* business, factory workers must be easy to get, but in *our* business talent combined with skill provides the geniuses we need to keep this place afloat!'

Andrew slammed the folder he was still holding down on to the table. Her cheeks, which had been flushed with her newfound fighting spirit, slowly paled.

'You smug little bitch!' The words were like a slap across her face and she actually blinked her eyes in a reflex motion. 'Have you forgotten why we're in this mess? Have you forgotten that not so very long ago you were caught with a campaign in your hands?'

His voice was raised in anger and several heads turned in their direction. One of the lead artists started towards them, his steps hesitant and unsure as he made his approach.

'Have you forgotten our truce?' snapped Jennifer. 'I thought we agreed not to fight in front of the staff.'

'Who's fighting?' Andrew asked in a snarl. 'I was merely reminding you of something you've apparently forgotten.'

The lead artist approached them now, his face red with embarrassment. His eyes fell on the folders and he seemed willing to leave them there. 'Er—the Corser campaign,' he muttered, as if this was the reason why he had come over.

Andrew snatched up the folders and placed them in the older man's arms. 'Here,' he said, making no attempt to put any friendliness into his tone. 'I've just been informed we have a two-week deadline to meet. Get started on these right away.'

The lead artist stared in amazement at the folders he found himself suddenly holding, thereby missing the charged look that passed between Jennifer and Andrew.

She watched Andrew leave the art room, black head held high and proud, the broad width of his shoulders suggesting he could carry anything, the forceful manner in which he walked telling the world it dared not cross him! Something inside Jennifer shivered as he very quietly shut the door behind him. She turned towards the lead artist, a smile pinned to her face. The artist looked from her to the door and he gave a sigh of relief. Jennifer knew what he meant. With Andrew gone, it was as if the cyclone had passed. Only she knew they were still in the eye of the storm!

'What was wrong with him?' asked the artist. 'Bad case of the nasties?'

'Oh,' she shrugged indifferently, 'that was just Andrew Thorpe being Andrew Thorpe.' She reached out to take the folders from him. 'These weren't meant for you,' she smiled. 'We've decided to give them to the junior artists!'

It was well past five when Jennifer returned to her own office to collect her bag and her jacket. Cheryle had packed up and gone home, and she savoured the few moments of peace and quiet before having to make her way down to the quay to catch the hydrofoil home.

She knew she had over stepped the mark by giving the campaign to the juniors, but she honestly believed they could do the job. She only hoped the work would be well on its way before Andrew got a whiff of it. And besides, she told herself, with Matt away she *was* the person in charge. So what if Andrew was the old man's son? It wasn't as if he actually worked here, he was more or less just a visitor.

Locking the door to her office, Jennifer crossed the reception area, her suit jacket over her arm and her bag slung across her shoulder. She felt tired, and the thought of the walk to the quay, followed by the trip on the hydrofoil, added to her weariness. The door to the reception area opened just as she approached it and she found herself facing Andrew. She started guiltily, thinking he must have found out about the campaign and had come to have it out with her. She braced herself for the arguments which she felt sure were to follow.

But Andrew, surprisingly, seemed in a mellow mood, and as she was beginning to become used to his flashpoint changes of temperament decided that either he didn't know she had given the work to the juniors or that he merely assumed she wouldn't dare! Either way he was relaxed, and she wasn't going to spoil anything by bringing up the subject.

'You're working late.' He smiled the words and she caught the faint odour of whisky on his breath, which probably explained his present easy manner, she thought.

'No later than usual,' she answered, trying to give the impression of being aloof and calm. Inwardly, her pulses were racing and her heart was skipping a wild tattoo against her ribs, reminding her somewhat painfully what his merest touch could do to her and that they were alone.

He was touching her now, his hand smoothing back the hair which had fallen against her cheek. His eyes held hers as he lowered his head to kiss her, his hand moving around her throat as he crushed the petal softness of her lips, drinking in their sweetness as though he still thirsted for wine. She pushed against him, her hands spreading across his chest as she struggled to escape. He grasped her hands in his, his long brown fingers curling around them, pinning them to his chest while he smiled down at her, a smile which was both seductive and cruel.

'Relax,' he drawled. 'The working day is finished, but the truce is still in effect.'

'You've been drinking!' she accused, glaring up at him.

He chuckled. 'Remarks like that remind me why I've never married. The thought of a nagging wife greeting me at the door makes my blood run cold!' He released her hands and she skittered away from him, holding her suit jacket in front of her as some sort of protection.

'And the thought of a drunk for a husband doesn't exactly turn me on either!' she flared.

They faced each other and the air seemed charged with electrical currents. Suddenly Andrew laughed. 'You should see what you look like—such dignity, such poise!' You remind me of a peahen who's just had her tail feathers plucked but is too proud to look behind to view the damage!'

Hot colour fused her cheeks. 'If that's an example of your sense of humour I find it lacking in hilarity!' She marched stiffly towards the door, her hand on the knob. 'Goodnight!'

Andrew walked beside her to the lift and she ignored the amused glances he bestowed on her. Downstairs he offered her a lift home.

'No thank you,' she returned primly. 'I think the hydrofoil would be a lot safer!'

'A glass of whisky, a small one at that, won't have affected my driving.' His smile was charming. 'Is it my driving you're afraid of, or is it me?'

She looked up and laughed in his face, and had the satisfaction of seeing the look of smug arrogance completely disappear. 'Afraid of you?' she scoffed, letting the laughter trickle slowly from her throat. 'Don't be absurd! You're nothing but a bully—a big, swaggering ape with a mouth to match!'

She held her ground bravely, her chin tilted in defiance as she watched him, fear making her insides turn to jelly. A car coming to an abrupt halt caused them both to turn around, and with immeasurable relief Jennifer saw the driver was Kevin. She raced towards the car and flung the door open, scampering inside and to safety.

As Kevin drove off she caught a fleeting glance of Andrew's face. The black scowl told her he would dearly have loved to kill her.

'What a blessing you came by when you did,' she told Kevin, her breathing coming in rapid gasps. 'Why did you?'

He shrugged. 'I was just passing. Who was that guy?'

'Andrew Thorpe, the old man's son.'

'A tyrant like his old man?' he slanted her a grin.

'A tyrant *un*like his old man,' she corrected with a smile. 'Just drop me off at the quay, Kevin.'

When Jennifer got home she paced around her flat. Why had she made it look as if she had been waiting for Kevin?—because she knew that that was what Andrew must have surely thought when she hurried into Kevin's car. She folded her arms across her chest. She had been afraid to let Andrew drive her home, not on account of his drinking, for she knew he had been far from drunk, but for what she thought might happen. She *might* have invited him in for a cup of coffee and he *might* have accepted. Would he have insisted on staying the night? Would she have had the will-power to insist he didn't? Was she more afraid of her own weakness than she was of his ability to make her as putty in his hands? Then suddenly she knew. It was his ability that caused her weakness. She was powerless against him.

Finally she made herself a snack. She wasn't hungry and the food seemed tasteless. She showered and changed into pyjamas, her thoughts solely centred on Andrew and the black mood he would surely be in the following morning. It wasn't until she walked down the small hallway leading to her bedroom that she saw the piece of paper which had been slipped under the front door. When she picked it up and read it, a frown crossed her face. The words printed were similar to the phone call.

Jennifer decided no matter what mood Andrew would be in in the morning, she must tell him about the telephone call and this note. She went into the lounge room and placed it in the top drawer of a bureau.

CHAPTER SEVEN

W<small>HEN</small> Jennifer arrived at work the next morning, Cheryle was already there, arranging long-stemmed yellow roses into a vase.

'Aren't these simply gorgeous?' she gushed, stepping back to admire them. 'Andrew dropped them in earlier. He said to give you a few if you wanted some.'

Jennifer took one of the roses from the vase. It reminded her of the one Andrew had brought to her flat the morning he had prepared breakfast. At the time she thought it had been a peace offering, but she had found out soon enough that it hadn't been. So now he was presenting Cheryle with roses and she wondered if it was for services rendered—then immediately felt ashamed of her thoughts.

'They're lovely, Cheryle,' she agreed, 'but please don't split them up.' How generous of Andrew, she thought meanly, to suggest to Cheryle to give her a few. As if she would accept a secondhand gift!

Jennifer went into her office and attempted to reach Andrew by phone, ringing practically every department of the agency, only to be told she had just missed him. Finally she decided to trace him by foot, thinking eventually their paths must cross.

As she crossed the reception area, Cheryle

stopped her. 'Oh, Miss Sloane,' she said, 'would you mind if I took a little longer for lunch today?' She cast dreamy eyes to the roses. 'Andrew has invited me.'

Jennifer's eyes widened in surprise, while her heart sank to the pit of her stomach.

'Andrew?' she asked weakly. 'You mean *Andrew Thorpe*?'

'Why, of course!' Cheryle bubbled her enthusiasm. 'Isn't he simply divine? I can't tell you how surprised I was when he invited me. I mean ... well, it sort of looked like he was interested in you. I never thought for an instant that it was *me* he liked!'

Jennifer found herself remembering how Andrew had held Cheryle's wrist, sniffing her perfume. The cad! Divine? No, she wouldn't describe Andrew Thorpe as being divine. Devious—that was more like it!

'Take as long as you like, Cheryle,' she said. 'I'm sure Andrew will get you back when he feels like it, not when you should be.'

Half an hour later, Jennifer finally came across Andrew in the mail room talking to one of the clerks. She waited until their conversation was finished before she crossed over to him. His eyes swept over her in a coldly cynical look, taking in the softly pleated blue silk blouse and the smooth lines of her skirt.

'No tailored business suit today, I see,' he bit out sarcastically. 'Going for the demure look?'

The question didn't merit an answer. He was obviously not in one of his better moods, and she felt it wise not to add fuel to the fire by deliberately goading him, which was what he was trying to do to her.

'I've been looking for you,' she said instead.

A black brow shot up. 'Why?'

'Because I must talk to you.'

His laugh was a snicker, and she watched in disbelief as he turned on his heel and deliberately walked away from her. She knew he would be angry about the night before, his black scowl had been fair enough warning, but she hadn't been prepared for absolute dismissal. She stalked after him, thankful they were in a little-used part of the mail room.

'Did you not hear me?' she asked when she caught up with him. 'I said I must talk to you. It's important, or at least I think it might be!' Her eyes flashed. 'Cheryle *loves* her roses.'

His eyes raked her face and she shivered under the impact of stormy black orbs. 'I should have thought all things of great importance would be for Kevin's ears. Why seek me out, when it's him you race to?' He ignored her remark about the roses, she noticed bitterly.

She dared a laugh. 'I thought you might be upset over last night, but I didn't think you would be upset enough to *sulk*! I mean, really Andrew, be fair. After all, you have Cheryle, why shouldn't Kevin have me? Or do you think just because you're the high and mighty Andrew Thorpe that you can have everything and everybody you damn well like?'

Her eyes were every bit as fiery as his own, and

she realised she had allowed herself to become
provoked when she had wanted to remain calm
and unflustered. She sorely regretted bringing
Cheryle into their conversation, thinking Andrew
would surely think she was jealous.

His mouth hardened into a cold thin line and his
eyes narrowed until they were mere slits. She had
never seen him look so cruel, and her breath
caught in her throat as she stared transfixed up at
him.

'Do you know where my father's office is?' he
asked in clipped, icy tones.

Jennifer could only nod.

'Meet me there in ten minutes—and for your
own good, don't be one second late!'

She went to his father's office immediately and
stood outside the door waiting for him. When half
an hour had gone by and he hadn't joined her, she
choked back her anger and decided to leave. If he
wanted to hear what she had to say, then he could
darn well look for her!

'Where are you going?' a curt voice behind her
asked.

She looked over her shoulder. Andrew was
making his way towards her, a sheaf of paper
tucked under his arm. He didn't wait for an
answer, nor did he look at her until he had
unlocked the door to his father's office. He
stepped aside, waiting for her to step through, and
Jennifer hesitated. She had made up her mind to
leave, and his surly attitude wasn't enticing her to
stay.

'I'm sorry,' she said, glancing at her watch. 'You

said ten minutes and it's been half an hour. I've got work to do and . . .'

He grabbed her arm and steered her into the office, effectively silencing her. She stood inside, her breath catching in her throat as she heard him shut the door behind them. She felt smothered by the hushed quietness of the room, with its thick pile carpeting and heavy curtains. Dark mahogany furniture littered the huge room and in the very centre was the deeply carved desk behind which the old man used to sit.

Jennifer watched Andrew cross the room and pull back the curtains. Immediately the room was flooded with light and she could see the room had been cared for despite the old man's absence. Not a speck of dust could be seen on any of the furniture, and despite its oppressiveness, the room had obviously been vacuumed and aired regularly. This knowledge made her feel glad, but she didn't give herself the chance to analyse her feelings, because her eyes were fastened on Andrew's sternly rigid form as he stood by the windows.

It was like going back in time when she had first walked into this office. She had been filled with nervous apprehension then, just as she was now. Andrew had been standing in exactly the same spot and she could vividly recall the old man with his snowy white hair sitting behind the desk. A ghost of a smile appeared on her lips. Would Andrew remember that this was where he had first called her Cinderella?

He turned from the windows to look at her and their eyes seemed to lock. 'Cinderella!' he said the name almost bitterly and she lowered her head, her small white teeth clenched at her bottom lip. She felt him watching her, then he walked over to the desk, the sound of the sheaf of papers he had been holding hitting the smooth surface, making her look up.

'I never dreamed when I called you by that name that I'd hit the nail so squarely on the head!' He was standing beside the desk, his long hands thrust into his pockets. 'It suited you then, as it does now,' he ended curtly.

'Whatever that means,' she answered quietly, head bent.

'You mean you don't know?' sarcastically.

Her eyes swept up to meet his face. It would be better to ignore his present antagonistic mood and she knew that any defiant reaction on her part would only serve to provoke him further. But she *wanted* to provoke him! Why should she let him walk all over her, needling her constantly with his barbed comments? An unreasonable anger flared within her and her eyes snapped at him, but her voice was smooth, pleasant even, as she said:

'And spoil all your fun by admitting that I do? It's obvious you're bursting at the seams to give me some garbled, nasty version of why you've called me by that name.'

His laugh was a low sneer. 'Cinderella the downtrodden; Cinderella the meek. That's how I once saw you.'

'But not now, of course.' How could she have ever been flattered by the name? she wondered bitterly. Downtrodden and meek! How horrible!

But then who wouldn't have been, in front of Andrew and his father?

'No, not now,' Andrew agreed, a sardonic smile slanting his mouth. 'Now I see you as an opportunist.'

'Really?' She reached up a slender hand to sweep back her blonde hair. 'I've grown in your estimation, then. Better an opportunist than downtrodden and meek.' She pretended to ponder this. 'Still, the meek shall inherit the earth.' She shot him a serious glance. '*Was* Cinderella an opportunist? I've never really thought about that, but then I'm not up on my fairy tales the way you so obviously are.'

His eyes narrowed dangerously and she wondered if she had gone too far. She lowered her head, smoothing the folds of her skirt.

'How was your date last night?' he asked suddenly, catching her off guard with the quick change of subject.

She gaped up at him, confusion lighting her eyes. 'Date?'

'With Kevin. Remember he rescued you, swept you off in his coach.'

'Oh, that,' she mumbled, guilt causing a deep flush to spread across her cheeks.

'Yes, *that*!' he snapped. 'Why didn't you tell me you had a date instead of making up all those wild excuses of why you didn't want me to drive you home?'

He had come over to stand by her chair and his anger flowed from him, covering her with a deep sense of dread. Nervously she licked her lips, knowing that if Andrew found out that she had only got Kevin to drive her to the quay he would regard it as an insult, especially if he knew that Kevin had happened along only by chance and that she had deliberately involved him as her means of escape from himself. His ego was such that she didn't dare dent it.

'Well?' The word cracked from his lips, and Jennifer snapped her head up to look at him. The light from the windows shone on his hair, making it appear more blue than black. Her lips parted at the sight, which was strangely beautiful, and her eyes were wide, fascinated. His eyes narrowed at that look, then he bent his head suddenly, catching her mouth in a searing kiss.

She didn't have time to react, it was over too fast for that, but the fiery demand of the smouldering impact of his mouth on hers left her shaken. Andrew straightened, towering over her, his face mocking. 'Just a little token of our friendship,' he told her coolly. 'Something to compare Kevin's kisses with!'

Flushed, she glared up at him, resisting the impulse to touch her mouth to feel if the impact of his kiss showed on it, as she felt it surely must. 'Are you sure you weren't comparing *Cheryle*'s kisses?' she returned angrily.

He had straightened, but now he bent towards her and she shrank from the cruelty visible in every line of his face and from the strong mouth twisted in a malicious curve. 'Let's leave Cheryle out of this, shall we?'

Jennifer lowered her eyes, deeply hurt by his

apparent desire to protect Cheryle. Satisfied that she had received his message, he once more straigtened, his eyes resting on the top of her shining fair hair. Her hurt festered into anger with an abruptness that caused her to tremble.

'No!' she flared, her voice quivering. 'Let's not leave Cheryle out of it! You feel you can say whatever you damn well please about Kevin and me, so let's discuss you and Cheryle for a change!' Angry sparks glittered in the bright green of her eyes as she impatiently flicked back the shining fall of her hair from flushed cheeks. 'For a start, the next time you invite her for lunch would you mind checking with me first?'

His incredulous bark of laughter only served to enrage her further, and her anger became out of all proportion when he said, 'You seem to have an inflated notion of your importance around here. Need I remind you . . .'

Jennifer jumped up, her hair cascading around her face, giving her an appearance of wildness. She was half crouched, her fists two tiny balls at her sides. 'Need I remind *you*,' she retorted, 'that we're running a business around here, *not* an escort agency! Everyone's on overtime as it is, and I don't think it was very considerate of you to ask my secretary to take an extended lunch hour. Now I'll be tied to my office, hardly able to get any work done while I perform her duties as well as my own.'

'If I didn't know how deeply you felt for Kevin I'd suggest you're jealous!'

That stopped her. She stared at him wide-eyed,

the fight leaving her body. 'Jealous?' she asked weakly. 'Don't be absurd.' She slumped into her chair. 'Concerned, yes, but jealous? Never!' Her eyes swept up to meet his glittering black gaze. 'And the only reason I'm concerned is because we're so behind in our campaigns. You're supposed to be the big man around her, at least for the moment, so I would have thought you would want to set an example.'

Andrew walked over to the desk and leaned against it, an insolent expression on his face. 'But that's how I choose to set an example,' he informed her coldly. 'Taking a secretary out to lunch is sort of a reward, wouldn't you agree? An incentive, if you like.'

If that was the only reason for taking Cheryle for lunch, then Jennifer didn't mind. But she couldn't help but wonder that if Cheryle didn't have the looks she had, would he still take her for lunch?

'If you're embarking on an incentive pro-gramme,' she couldn't resist saying, 'then it looks like every one of your lunch breaks are going to be spent with a member of the staff. I can't think of a single person here who doesn't deserve a reward, or who wouldn't jump at the chance to dine with the high and mighty Andrew Thorpe!'

'Can't you?' he drawled, his eyes blazing into her own. 'Well, I can think of at least one!'

She lowered her eyes, feeling hot colour sear her cheeks. 'I . . . suppose you'll be taking Cheryle to that seaside restaurant down by the quay?' The one he had taken her to.

'No, not that one,' he answered glibly. 'Cheryle prefers Italian food to seafood. We'll go to a nice quiet Italian restaurant. There's a new one just opened at Kings Cross.'

'I'm sure you'll both enjoy yourselves,' she remarked, rising to her feet and starting for the door. Andrew was beside her in an instant.

'You haven't told me yet why you wanted to see me.' He reminded her of the reason why they were in his father's office. She had completely forgotten about the telephone call and the scrap of paper which had been slipped under her door. Somehow, it had lost its importance, and she didn't feel up to discussing it.

'It wasn't important,' she answered, her hand on the knob of the door.

Andrew leaned against the door, making it impossible for her to open. She glared up at him, detesting his look of smug arrogance.

'It was important enough for you to come looking for me,' he pointed out, smiling at her stiff attitude. 'Didn't you want to apologise to me?'

She could only gape at him. 'Apologise?' she croaked. 'Apologise to *you*? Whatever for, may I be so bold as to ask?'

'Perhaps apologise was the wrong word. Silly of me to think it might be in your vocabulary! Try confession. Don't you have something you want to confess to me?'

'The only thing I can confess to is that I'm confused. What are you talking about?'

'The campaign you gave to the juniors!' He

placed his hand on her arm and she tried to ignore the tingling sensation that swept through her.

'Oh, that,' she mumbled.

'Ah, the light shines!' His hand moved caressingly up to her shoulder. 'Don't worry about it,' and she thought, how big of him. 'They're doing a great job,' just like she said they would. 'I'll keep an eye on them.' Interfere would be more like it! But wisely she said nothing, grateful he at least couldn't read her thoughts. But when he held open the door for her, he had a funny little smile on his mouth, causing her to wonder if he in fact could and had read them.

Cheryle was typing madly when Jennifer got back to her office, making Jennifer wonder how many typing errors were being made. Half an hour later Andrew came to collect Cheryle, and Jennifer's heart contracted at the incredibly handsome pair they made. She had meant to be somewhere near her office at lunchtime, but work had dealyed her. Now she was forced to watch the happy couple make their departure.

'Enjoy yourselves,' she said, hoping her voice sounded cheerful, noncommittal. It didn't. Her eyes caught Andrew's and she flushed at his deeply mocking look.

'Care to join us?' he surprised her by asking, much to Cheryle's consternation.

'Good heavens, no!' Jennifer denied, managing to make the invitation sound like a fate worse than death. 'I'll probably ring Kevin and have a sandwich with him.'

Andrew's eyes ignited with spontaneous fury.

'Yes, why don't you?' he snapped, before steering Cheryle out of the reception area and banging the door shut behind them.

It wasn't until after they had gone that Jennifer realised her knees were shaking. She became angry with herself for allowing Andrew to have such an effect on her nervous system. The only remedy she knew to keep him off her mind was to bury herself in work. She had no intention of having lunch with Kevin, she had only said that to get Andrew's goat.

She worked through her lunch hour. She worked through the afternoon tea break. She worked until past five o'clock. When five-thirty came and Andrew still hadn't returned her secretary, she was furious. Finally she packed up and went home.

The first thing she noticed when she got home was that there was a new doorman. They nodded to each other, but Jennifer didn't stop to enquire what had happened to the regular doorman. Once inside her lovely flat she changed out of her working clothes and into slacks and top. She felt too keyed up to eat, so after pouring herself a glass of juice she went out on to her balcony to drink it. Downstairs the new doorman looked up, saw her there and turned sharply away.

Jennifer decided she didn't much like him. The old doorman had been much nicer, jovial. This one had a rather sinister look to his tightly closed up features. Her eyes focused on the harbour, skimming across the water to pick up the distant shapes of Sydney's skyscrapers. Somewhere in that throbbing metropolis were Andrew and Cheryle. Where had they gone after lunch? she wondered bleakly. Had they driven up the coast, perhaps for a swim or to sightsee? Had Cheryle invited him back to her place? What were they doing? What had they done? Perhaps they were at a night club, dancing, holding each other.

Her hand holding the glass was trembling, causing the liquid to spill on to the tiles of her balcony. Angry with herself for her jealous thoughts, she went into the kitchen and returned to the balcony with a cloth to wipe up the spilt juice. It was getting dark now, lights were twinkling and the harbour took on a carnival atmosphere. Her telephone rang.

Her whole body stiffened. It wasn't until she heard it ring that she admitted she had been waiting for that sound. She crossed the room to answer it, blood rushing to her temples. But it wasn't Andrew as she had hoped, it was Kevin, and she tried to conceal her bitter disappointment by sounding overly cheerful. Kevin, on the other hand, sounded strangely morose and made no attempt to hide it.

'What's wrong?' asked Jennifer at last.

'Just one of those days,' he admitted dismally.

'I know what you mean,' she agreed on a sigh.

'Have you had dinner?'

'No, not yet. I've barely got home.'

'How about if I come around?' he suggested hopefully.

'All right,' she agreed without enthusiasm.

'Don't bother cooking anything,' he told her. 'I'll bring a pizza.'

An hour later Kevin arrived with the pizza and a bottle of wine. The delicious aroma of the pizza reminded Jennifer that she hadn't eaten since breakfast. She got out plates and sliced the pizza on to them while Kevin opened the wine and poured it into two glasses. They made short work of their dinner and after clearing away the dishes settled in the lounge room with cups of coffee.

'How's work going?' Kevin asked her.

'Hectic. We're way behind with our campaigns.'

'Surely things must be better with Andrew on the scene?'

'He's made a lot of changes,' she nodded, staring into her coffee. 'Some people consider them radical, while others think they're long overdue.'

'And you?' he asked casually. 'What do you think?'

She looked up from her coffee cup and smiled. 'I wouldn't admit it to him for the world, but I agree with all of them. He's brilliant as far as business goes.'

'You sound as though you like him.'

'Oh, he's all right. A bit too arrogant for his own good, though. He likes everything his own way,' said Jennifer mournfully.

'Just like his old man,' Kevin agreed testily, reaching into his pocket for his cigarettes. The light was shining on his hair and casting a shadow across his face. Compared to Andrew he lacked significance, Jennifer decided without being unkind. His fair hair seemed so thin and lifeless compared to Andrew's thick black scrub. Even his eyes were really too pale to be attractive and his mouth was small and poutish.

'I always liked Andrew's father,' she defended the old man. 'I never really got the chance to know him well, but I saw enough of him to know I liked him.'

Kevin lit a cigarette and watched the smoke curl in the air. Jennifer got up and opened a window to allow the smoke to escape. Outside she could see the doorman, and at that instant he turned and stared up at her as though he had been watching her apartment all along. She quickly stepped back and drew the curtains. She had the peculiar sensation that the new doorman was spying on her!

'More coffee?' she asked Kevin, crossing over to pick up the coffee pot.

'I have plenty, thanks,' he smiled, indicating his cup which she had filled moments ago. He watched her closely. 'What's wrong with you tonight, Jen? You're coiled up tighter than a spring. Sit down and relax,' he coaxed her, as she stood rubbing her arms as though to get the blood circulating.

Jennifer flopped into a chair and smiled across at him. Dear Kevin, she thought. He was really the best friend she had, and she wondered what he would say if she were to tell him that Andrew suspected them both of being thieves. Andrew! If she was coiled up like a spring, Andrew was to blame. She had admitted she was jealous of Andrews's attentions to Cheryle, but admitting to something didn't alleviate the pain. Had their date finally ended? She sighed deeply and stood up—it was impossible to remain sitting—and then at the look Kevin gave her, reluctantly sat back down again.

Kevin chuckled. 'I've never seen you like this. You're usually so calm and cool. Want to tell me about it?'

'Oh, it's just work,' she hedged. 'We've got the junior artists working on a campaign.'

'The Corser Car Care Products?'

'Yes, but how did you know?' she asked, surprised.

He hesitated, reaching for his cup. 'You told me,' he ventured finally.

'But I couldn't have,' she protested. 'They only started yesterday . . .'

'What does it matter?' he interrupted. 'God, Jen, I think you need a holiday. You haven't been yourself lately.'

She watched him light another cigarette. 'You smoke too much, Kevin,' she mumbled. 'I thought you were trying to cut down.'

He inhaled deeply, watching her. 'You're becoming a real nag.'

Jennifer flushed deeply. Andrew had accused her of the same thing. Perhaps Kevin was right and she did need a holiday. A holiday from men, one man in particular, she thought hotly. Perhaps she was becoming a nag, she thought miserably as she cleared away the coffee cups and carried the tray into the kitchen.

Returning to the lounge, she watched Kevin. He was stretched in the chair, his legs out in front of him, an arm tossed over the side of his chair and a cigarette dangling dangerously from his fingers. Suddenly he irritated her and she wanted nothing more than for him to leave.

'Kevin,' she said from the doorway, 'it's getting late and I'm tired. Would you mind leaving, please—I'd like to get to bed.'

'Hey, come on!' he laughed, straightening in his chair and glancing at his watch. 'It's barely nine-thirty!'

'I know, but I'm tired, and tomorrow promises to be another hectic day. I'd really like to get to bed early.'

Kevin's eyes narrowed thoughtfully. 'This Andrew Thorpe must mean more to you than you're willing to admit. You've never kicked me out this early before,' he accused.

'I'm sorry, Kevin,' she sighed. 'I'm not being rude or anything, it's just as I said . . . I'm tired.'

'All right, I can take a hint.' He got up and walked towards the door, Jennifer following him. At the door he turned to her. 'The smartest thing I ever did was to get out of that agency,' he rasped. 'I hated that place!'

Surprised by the vehemence in his voice, Jennifer stared at him. 'I know you never enjoyed working at the agency, Kevin, but I never realised you hated it.' She put her hand on his arm. 'Don't you ever miss it . . . even a little?'

'Why would I? I've got my own business, I'm my own boss. Look at you . . . you're tired out, or so you say. Yet tomorrow you have to face up to more of the same.' He reached behind and opened the door, smiling at her. 'And I'm willing to bet Andrew Thorpe expects to be handled with kid gloves, just like his old man always insisted on.' The smile turned into a sneer. 'It must be more than they can bear to have their campaigns ripped off right in front of their aristocratic noses!'

The next morning, Jennifer tried very hard to act natural around Cheryle, but it was tough going. She was in love with Andrew, but it was Cheryle he had dated. How to behave naturally around a woman who had had an extended luncheon with the man she adored was about the hardest thing Jennifer felt she had ever had to do.

Was she being overly polite, she kept asking herself, or was she being too nonchalant? Several times she caught Cheryle passing her curious glances, so then she tried harder than ever to maintain an aura of strict business procedures. She dictated several letters, held appointments, conversed with the Art Department. At eleven-thirty Cheryle told her she was leaving for lunch.

'I shouldn't be too late, though,' Cheryle said. 'Andrew said we'd just grab a quick snack.'

Jennifer stared at her. 'You mean you're going for lunch with ... with Andrew *again*?' she asked incredulously.

'Yes, isn't it wonderful?' Cheryle simpered. 'I've never known a man like him before. He's just so ... so manly.' She reached into her drawer and pulled out her perfume. 'Andrew loves this,' she explained as she splashed it on.

'He certainly must,' muttered Jennifer, watching the operation in awe. She glanced at Cheryle's desk, at the letters which hadn't been typed, at the filing basket next to overflowing. Yesterday's work hadn't been done, and now it looked as though today's work didn't stand much of a chance either.

'Cheryle,' she said, 'when do you think you're going to find time to catch up with your work? Those letters I dictated this morning . . . I told you they were important, but I notice you haven't even started on them yet.'

Cheryle flicked them a quick and careless look. 'Andrew said if I got behind to take the work down to the typing pool.'

'Oh, he did, did he?' Jennifer bit out. 'I hope you told him that none of our work goes to the typing pool, that it's all highly confidential.'

Cheryle shrugged and was about to answer when Andrew walked into the reception area dressed in a smart grey business suit, the tanned column of his neck showing smoothly above the crisp white of his shirt. He looked from Jennifer to Cheryle, a roguish smile on his mouth.

'Ready?' he asked Cheryle, and Jennifer watched with an ache in her heart as the girl smiled up at him, her dark eyes shining.

'Yes, but Jennifer is concerned about the letters I haven't typed,' she pouted, looking across at Jennifer.

It was the first time Cheryle had ever referred to her by her christian name, and Jennifer felt anger swelling in her throat. Cheryle seemed to be having a personality change, and obviously Andrew was the one directly responsible.

Andrew glanced at Jennifer with an unreadable

expression in his eyes. 'I told Cheryle to send anything she couldn't handle down to the typing pool,' he told her, and Jennifer felt her cheeks fuse with colour.

'Yes, Cheryle mentioned that you'd said something like that, but unfortunately it can't be done. You see, our work is on the highest level and we like to practise top security. That's why Matt and I have a *private* secretary,' she pointed out, her eyes narrowed as she glared at him. 'Our work is private!'

Andrew's smile was slow in forming. 'If there's something . . . anything that can't wait, I suggest you type it up yourself.' He steered Cheryle to the door. 'You do type, don't you?'

Jennifer was livid with rage, her green eyes snapping. 'Yes,' she managed through stiff lips, 'but that's not the . . .'

'I thought you might,' Andrew interrupted as he opened the door for him and Cheryle. 'Just do the ones that are most important,' he flung over his shoulder before shutting the door after them.

Jennifer controlled a wild impulse to throw something, anything. She sat down at Cheryle's desk, wondering how Andrew could have humiliated her in such a way in front of Cheryle.

She looked gloomily at the tapes, wondering if her typing was good enough to do a few letters. After several attempts it all came back to her and by three o'clock she had the most important letters ready for the late afternoon mail. She hadn't had lunch by the time Cheryle returned at three-thirty.

She waved Cheryle's apologies aside and went

down to the cafeteria for a sandwich and a cup of tea. Andrew was standing in front of the water cooler when she passed by on her way back up to her office. He appeared to be deep in conference, and she was glad to be able to slip past him without being seen by him or the three employees he was speaking with.

He caught up with her while she was waiting for the lift.

'How did the typing go?' he had the nerve to ask.

'Fine,' she answered without looking at him.

'Jill of all trades, eh?'

'Someone has to be,' she answered flippantly.

'Meaning?' She could hear the laughter in his voice.

'Meaning that I shall have to get a new secretary if you're going to be constantly taking Cheryle from her work.' She hunched away from him, away from his disturbing closeness. 'You must find Cheryle fascinating company, to keep her away so long.'

'She is, rather,' he agreed warmly, and Jennifer's heart seemed to drop to the pit of her stomach. 'But so are you, in your own snappish little way!' His hand reached out to touch her cheek. 'I won't be at work tomorrow. I'll pick you up at two o'clock Saturday.'

Her eyes swept up to meet his mocking glance.

'You haven't forgotten about our date, have you?' he enquired softly. 'I'm taking you to visit Dad, remember?'

She hadn't forgotten. She had only thought he had.

CHAPTER EIGHT

JENNIFER dressed with great care for her date on Saturday with Andrew. An afternoon spent with Andrew and his father just had to be more important than a mere lunch, she told herself. She was up early, had a swim in the surf, showered and shampooed her hair, brushing it until it fell in shining waves across her shoulders.

At half past one she slipped into a pair of white slacks with a pale mauve top. Small white sandals were on her feet. Dressed and ready, she sat down to wait, her heart pattering as if it had a thousand tiny birds in its cage. Her anticipation was such that when the doorbell rang at precisely two o'clock she jumped from her chair as though shot from a gun. Hurrying towards it, she flung it open with a grand flourish, unaware that an eager, happy smile curved her lips.

Andrew stood there looking down at her, his eyes resting on the unguarded look of happiness in her eyes, the shy but welcoming smile on the sweet curve of her mouth. He was dressed casually in a pair of blue jeans and a red T-shirt, but even dressed so casually he still managed to maintain an air of well-bred elegance, and her heart caught in her throat at the incredibly handsome picture he made.

His lips parted in a lazily sensuous smile as his

eyes wandered down the length of her body,
causing her heart to skip crazily in her chest.

'I've been waiting for you,' she heard herself
say, then immediately regretted her impulsiveness
as a wicked gleam settled in his eyes.

'Missed me, have you?' he drawled, stepping in
and kicking the door shut behind him. His hand
reached out to cup her chin, forcing her head back
so that he could see her eyes.

'Y-yes,' she stammered, mesmerised by the
potency of his glittering black gaze.

His hand moved behind the sweep of her hair.
'You shouldn't answer your door without checking
to see who it is first,' he told her, drawing her
close.

'I . . . I know,' she managed to murmur as he
lowered his head to nuzzle one fiery red earlobe.
'B-but I knew it would be you.'

His arms locked around her, moulding her to
his length. Desire flooded her body and as she
gazed helplessly up at him, she knew by the look in
his eyes that he was perfectly aware of the
upheaval his closeness was doing to her weakening
senses. His mouth trailed to her lips and she parted
her mouth in eager expectation of his kiss, his lips
drinking in their sweetness like a man dying of
thirst.

She strained against him, shivering in delight as
his hands roamed freely over the curves of her
body. She forgot all the insults, all the hurts, all
the wild accusations. Andrew's hands made her
forget, his expertise as a lover would ensure she
would remember him long after he had forgotten

her. But she didn't care. Only the present mattered. She was like jelly in his arms, putty that he could mould and do with whatever he pleased. She didn't care. Beyond this moment there weren't any others.

The telephone rang, and the harshness of the sound brought her back to sanity with an abruptness that caused her to jerk violently. Andrew cursed and walked over to pick it up.

'Hullo ... hullo.' He turned to face her, the phone in his hands, and she knew by the look on his face that the caller had hung up. He replaced the receiver, a frown wrinkling his brow. 'That's strange,' he said, looking across at her. 'Have you been having trouble with your telephone?'

Dazed from their lovemaking and from the abruptness of having it suddenly stopped, Jennifer could only shake her head.

Andrew looked down at the phone, a frown still on his brow. 'There were some strange sounds,' he said slowly. 'Clapping sounds and then a hissing noise.'

His words got through to her and she remembered the call she had taken in Matt's office. Her eyes widened in surprise. 'I had a call similar to that in Matt's office,' she told him, her eyes travelling from his face to the telephone. 'Was there any sort of message?'

He crossed over to her. 'What do you mean by "message"?' he asked her quietly.

Jennifer shrugged. 'I'm really not quite sure. It was sort of garbled, hard to make out, but it sounded like "Keep away from there".' Colour rose to her cheeks. Repeating it aloud made it sound rather ludicrous, disbelieving.

Andrew's eyes narrowed shrewdly. 'When did you get this call?'

'I think it was Monday. Yes, it was Monday afternoon, shortly after we returned from lunch. At first I wasn't going to answer it because it was on Matt's special line.'

'Did you recognise the voice, or anything else which might have sounded familiar?'

'No, and I'm not even sure if what I heard was correct. Nothing about the call was very clear.' She looked up at him, trying to guess what he was thinking. 'I wouldn't worry about it,' she said. 'It's probably just some kid playing a prank.'

His eyes studied her face, then he turned away from her crossing to the window. He stood in silence and she could tell by his posture that she had somehow managed to anger him. Suddenly he turned, thrusting his hand into his pocket. 'And these?' he asked. 'Are these some sort of prank as well?'

She stared at the two little black combs in his hand. 'My combs! Where did you find them?' she gasped. 'I've been looking for them.'

She watched as his hand closed over them, then he shoved them back into his pocket. 'You'll never guess!' he bit out.

'I'd put them in my desk drawer, but when I went to get them, they were gone,' Jennifer told him.

Andrew crossed over to her. 'I found them in Matt's safe!'

'What!' She felt the pressure of his hands on her shoulders. 'But you couldn't have! I remember putting them in my desk.'

'I went to the office last night to do some work,' he told her. 'I needed some things from Matt's safe. As soon as I had it opened I saw your combs. They were sticking out of the latest campaign folder.'

Behind her was a chair, and she sank into it. 'Someone must have put them there,' she offered weakly, not daring to look up at him.

Andrew gave a loud snort. 'Brilliant deduction!'

Her green eyes snapped to his face. 'Well, it wasn't me! God, you don't think I'd be so daft as to leave my combs behind if I were the thief!'

He dragged a hand through his hair. 'Tell me more about that phone call.'

'There's nothing more to tell. It was over so quickly I hardly had a chance to make it out.'

'When Cheryle put the call through, did you ask her if the caller had identified himself? He must have had to sound normal, otherwise she wouldn't have carried through with it.'

Jennifer shook her head. 'Cheryle wasn't at her desk. She was at Printing.'

His breath came out in a loud sigh. 'There was no one around then? You were alone in the office?'

Jennifer stirred uncomfortably. 'Yes.'

'Either you have nerves of steel or you're downright stupid! Why didn't you report the call to me?'

'Because I knew you would only insult me if I did,' she retorted angrily.

He leaned towards her and she shrank from his murderous glare. 'We've had a thief operating for quite some time now and you worry about insults?' He straightened and she knew he was having difficulty getting his anger under control. 'Have you discussed the thefts with anyone?' he asked.

'No, I hardly see anyone outside the Agency.'

'What about Kevin? You see enough of him.' His voice was accusing. 'Do you talk about work matters, or are your conversations more on the social level?'

Anger sparked in her eyes. 'If you think I'm going to discuss my relationship with Kevin then you're sadly mistaken!'

He grabbed her roughly from the chair and shook her. 'I'm in no mood for games,' he snarled. 'Unless you have something to hide I suggest you answer my questions.' He released her and she staggered back against the chair.

'Of course I discuss work matters with Kevin,' she said angrily. 'Why wouldn't I? He understands about the Agency and the problems we face.'

'So you've kept him informed about the thefts? Let him in on all our plans? Told him which campaigns we're working on?'

'I've mentioned the thefts,' she answered heatedly, 'but I've never gone into detail—Kevin would find that boring. He's not particularly interested in what goes on at the Agency. That's why he quit. He hated the place.'

His eyes roamed her face. 'Enough to see it ruined?'

Shocked, she could only stare at him. 'I've told you before, Kevin is *not* the thief. He couldn't be.'

'Why? Because he's your lover? Because he's the man of your dreams, your hope for the future?'

Colour scorched her cheeks. 'No,' she answered quietly.

'No, what?' he snapped. 'No, he's not your lover?'

She eyed him evenly. 'No, he's not the *thief*!'

Andrew's face darkened with new fury and his eyes became Satan's eyes. The devil she thought she had unleashed in him before was as nothing compared to now. His body shook as if he were in sudden agony and his breathing came in torturous gasps. Jennifer stared at him, and he stared back as if he did not see her at all. He took a step towards her and she didn't move, dumbfounded by his reaction.

His hands reached out and she felt them around her throat. She squeezed her eyes shut, then she felt his hands slide away as he pushed her away from him. Her eyes flew open and she was further shocked by his appearance, as though he had suddenly aged. His shoulders were slumped and his face was deeply lined and haggard. She watched him fight for control.

Their silence was measured and seemed terrible. It was as though each was waiting for the other to move to give excuse for pursuit. Jennifer remained rigid. She was terrified of moving a muscle in case his control snapped. Finally he passed a hand across his eyes, and when he looked at her she sighed in relief. Whatever had happened to him had safely passed, and he was back to his normal, obnoxiously arrogant self.

'Your Friday night boy-friend shows up on a Wednesday night. Didn't you find that rather strange?'

Jennifer lowered herself into her chair, weakness flooding her body. 'How did you know?' she asked.

'Never mind how I know. Just answer my question.'

'No, I didn't find that strange,' she answered, not looking at him. 'Kevin rang and I invited him over for dinner.'

His silence was oppressive, but she didn't dare risk looking at him.

'What did you talk about?' he asked at last.

She bit back a sharp retort. 'Not much. Hardly anything, in fact.'

'He arrived shortly after you got home from work and didn't leave until after nine-thirty. What were you doing the whole time, if you weren't talking?' Sarcastically.

It didn't surprise her that he knew the exact times of Kevin's visit. What did surprise her was how he knew.

'Obviously you were spying on us, so perhaps you can tell me!' Her murderous glare matched his. 'You left out that Kevin brought a pizza with him.'

'A pizza *and* a bottle of wine,' he informed her coolly.

'Well, now you have your answer,' she quipped. 'That's what Kevin and I were doing—eating and drinking.'

He shoved his hands into his pockets. 'Would it be safe to assume you didn't receive any peculiar phone calls while Kevin was here?'

'Extremely safe. We didn't.'

He eyed her coldly. 'Don't push me, Jennifer. I've told you before I don't take kindly to provocation.'

'And I don't take kindly to being spied upon, nor do I like my guests being spied upon.'

Andrew's smile was faintly malicious. 'I'm not particularly concerned with your likes or dislikes. What I am concerned with is the leakage of information from the Agency.'

'And do you think I'm not?' Tears of frustration and indignation filled her eyes, making them appear more startlingly green. 'My God, Andrew, can't you see I'm as concerned as you are?' Her voice caught and she turned her head away from him, wiping at her eyes at the same time.

He reached her, his hands surprisingly gentle as he brought her to her feet, but she refused to look up at him, her eyes level with his chest. He tilted her chin up, his eyes hardening at the sight of her tears. Then he crushed her to him and she felt her breath being squeezed from her body.

'Do you know what you're doing to me?' he asked her hoarsely, his voice ragged, filled with pain. Mercifully, his arms relaxed and she was able to regain her breath, but he still held her pinned against his chest and she felt the rapid thumping of his heart. Then with a strangled moan he released her, her eyes staring up at him in a sort of breathless wonder. She shook her head helplessly, folding her hands in front of her.

'Would ... you like some coffee?' she asked after a moment.

His laugh was bitter. 'Coffee?' he repeated. 'You think that might help, do you? Well, I'm afraid it won't.'

'I was only trying to be polite!' she returned stiffly.

His eyes searched her face, then he shrugged. 'Make some for yourself.' He moved away from her, once more going to stand in front of the window. When he turned she was still there, watching him.

'Well?' Andrew raised a darkly quizzical brow. 'Aren't you going to make coffee?'

'I don't want any,' she answered. 'I only thought you might.' When he didn't answer she ventured to ask, 'Shouldn't we be going?'

'Soon,' he growled, and under his scrutiny she became nervously shy. Her eyes skimmed around the room aware of his eyes watching her. Her gaze settled on the antique bureau, and suddenly she remembered the scrap of paper which had been thrust under her door.

'I haven't told you about another message I received,' she blurted, pathetically grateful to have something to divert his attention with.

'What other message?'

'It was a note,' she rushed to tell him. 'Similar in words to the phone call.

He frowned. 'When did you receive this? At work?'

'No ... no. Here at home.'

'When?'

'Monday night. Someone slipped it under my door.'

'Someone slipped a note under your door and you didn't bother mentioning it to anyone?' Andrew's eyes were disbelieving.

'But I tried to tell ... someone,' she answered, shaken by his tone.

'Who?' he snapped. Kevin?'

'No. As a matter of fact I tried to tell you on Tuesday morning, but you were your usual unapproachable self. I think you might remember our little meeting in your father's office?'

'Well, for God's sake don't stand there like a stupid little bitch,' he roared. 'Get me the damned note!'

'I won't!' she yelled back, surprising him. 'Not unless you apologise for calling me those foul names!'

'You're in no position to bellow at me,' he warned her with a snarling rage. 'Now if you have a note ... *get it!*'

She stood her ground, her chin quivering. 'Ask me nicely.'

There was a stunned silence. 'Jennifer, would you please get that note?' he asked after a moment.

She turned on her heel and marched stiffly towards the bureau. Opening it, she rummaged inside. Andrew came to stand beside her.

'What's the matter?' he growled. 'Can't you find it?'

'It's got to be here somewhere,' she answered, frantically searching for it. But when everything had been taken from the drawer and put back again, she had to admit the note wasn't there. She turned slowly to stare up at Andrew, dread mingled with fear lighting her eyes. 'It's gone! Somebody's taken it!' Kevin, she thought. No one else had been in her home. Had he taken it when she was in the kitchen clearing up? No! No! She was allowing Andrew to warp her thinking. Kevin didn't even know she had the note.

Andrew frowned, watching her. 'Are you sure this is where you put it?'

'Yes ... yes, I remember distinctly.' She shivered, her eyes filled with uneasiness as she looked around the room.

'That settles it. You're not staying here a minute longer. I want you to pack a bag. You can stay with Dad until this whole rotten mess gets cleared up.' He grabbed her arm, steering her towards her bedroom. 'Pack enough for a couple of weeks.'

'But I can't,' she protested, trying to struggle out of his grip. 'I can't just leave my home ...'

Andrew dragged her into the bedroom. 'You'll do as you're told!' Jennifer fell against him and his arms fastened around her, like rigid coils of steel. His face was barely inches from hers, a very disturbing closeness which was doing strange things to her heart.

Was he going to kiss her? She shivered in expectation and he smiled down at her upturned face as though he had guessed her thought. His eyes held hers and for a split second all the universe came to a halt, then exploded into trillions of fragments as his mouth came crashing down on hers.

It wasn't a pleasant kiss. His mouth was hard and bruising and she knew he was making a deliberate attempt to hurt her, to punish her for her loyalty to Kevin. She tried to wriggle out of his arms, but too late she realised her mistake. No one escaped from Andrew Thorpe that easily. She felt his hand move up to her head and a muffled sound escaped her mouth as her hair was gripped cruelly and pulled back. 'Keep still,' he warned, then his mouth was on hers again, forcing her lips apart. Fire lit her veins. Her arms crept up his back and her fingers stroked through the thick mass of his hair. She was hardly aware that he had pulled her blouse loose. All she knew was the thrillingly exciting feel of his hands on her bare flesh. She arched closer to him and she felt him unclasp her bra, his hands cupping her breasts.

'Oh, Jennifer,' he whispered against her ear, his lips nuzzling the soft lobes as his hands continued their onslaught on her slender yielding body. He picked her up and carried her to the bed, gently laying her down, before stretching out beside her. He unbuttoned her blouse, removing it and her bra, exposing the creamy silkiness of her firm young breasts. His hands gently cupped her breasts, his thumbs caressing the rosy peaks. She stared helplessly into his face, her eyes a smoky green and her cheeks deeply flushed. She was powerless to stop him. Andrew bent his head and kissed her, and she opened her mouth obediently to become his passive slave. She didn't resist when he pulled her slacks off or when he unbuckled his belt and slid out of his jeans. She knew what was surely to follow, but God help her, she did nothing to stop him.

Andrew took his time. He was an expert lover. His mouth went from one small breast to the other, his lips gently nuzzling the erected peaks. Her small hands pressed against his back, willing him to relieve her of this exquisite torture. She felt him ease himself on top of her and his arms slid under her back. 'God, Jennifer,' he groaned against her ear, 'I've dreamed of this since the first time I set eyes on you.' His mouth strayed to hers and she met his kiss with fiery demand.

Afterwards he lay beside her, gently stroking her hair. Her lips were swollen from their love and the dark fringe of her lashes framed the sweet innocence of her startling green eyes. Her lips parted in a smile as she reached up to run her fingers lightly over the smooth line of his jaw. How she loved him, and how she yearned to hear him say that he loved her! He reached for her hand and brought it to his lips, tenderly kissing each fingertip. While her own eyes were shining with love, his were dark with regret.

'What's wrong?' she whispered softly, puzzled by his look. 'Have I done something to upset you?'

Andrew moaned and drew her close, his lips against the curve of her breasts. 'How could you upset any man?' he said. 'Your body was made for love, but I swear, Jennifer, I never meant for this to happen. Not yet.'

Disappointment and regret at his words made her stiffen. 'B-but you liked it, didn't you?' she asked in bewilderment.

He leaned over her, smiling at her words. 'Of course I *liked* it. You were perfect, but I never dreamed for an instant that you were still a virgin. I really thought that you and Kevin . . .' His words trailed off and he shrugged his shoulders, while Jennifer stared up at him in disbelief.

'I don't believe this,' she said stiffly, her eyes mirroring her hurt, as she struggled into a sitting position, grabbing the coverlet to hide her breasts. 'Love had nothing to do with . . . with what we just did, did it?' she stammered the words, her cheeks glowing hot with shame as she realised he had only been using her. 'You just wanted from me what you thought Kevin was getting!' Tears of outrage sparkled in her eyes. 'How could you be so cruel?' she gasped. 'S-so heartless!'

Andrew got up from the bed and tossed her her clothes. 'Get dressed,' he ordered, as he reached for his jeans, sliding his long legs into them. He glared menacingly at her. 'You and Kevin are of age,' he said cruelly. 'It was natural to assume you'd slept together. Now that I know you haven't, make sure you never do!'

Her cheeks were crimson. 'I see,' she lashed back. 'I'm your own special property now, am I? Well, sorry to disappoint you, because I'm not and I never will be.' She gulped back her tears of heartbreak. 'Don't think this has been a special moment for me, because it hasn't. I . . . I was looking for someone to make love to me because . . . because I wanted to see what it was like.'

Andrew was standing in front of her, his legs

slightly apart as he buckled his belt. He smiled at her words, his hands resting lightly on his belt buckle. Tears sparkled like tiny jewels along her lashes. 'If I thought that was true,' he said, his hands tightening on his belt, 'I'd beat you within an inch of your life.' A hand snaked out and ripped away the coverlet and she squealed in protest, crossing her arms across her breasts to hide her shameful nakedness from his lecherous eyes. His smile was slightly malicious as he pulled her from the bed. 'Get dressed,' he told her again. He looked around the room. 'Where do you keep your suitcases?'

Jennifer prayed for death, for anything that would take her from this room and out of his sight. Gingerly she reached down and grabbed for the coverlet, expecting at any moment that he would snatch it from her. 'In that cupboard over there,' she half pointed, grateful that his attention could be averted elsewhere. As he strode towards the cupboard, she grabbed her clothes and ran into the bathroom, shutting and locking the door after her.

A quick shower made her feel a little better, and after dressing and putting on some make-up, she summoned up the courage to step back into her bedroom. She ignored Andrew as she walked over to her bed, straightening the covers and folding the coverlet at the bottom. She pretended not to see that he had already packed her suitcases, but it disgusted her to know that he had handled her frilly underthings.

'Ready?' he asked, picking up a case in either hand.

Jennifer didn't answer, and it gave her a small amount of pleasure when she saw a look of annoyance cross his features. Marching stiffly in front of him, with her head held high, she stopped at her front door. With her hand on the knob, she turned to face him. 'I'll have you know I'm doing this under protest,' she told him, her eyes flashing in defiance. 'If any of my plants die from lack of water, which they surely will, I shall hold you personally responsible.'

She missed his smile as she turned to open the door. Downstairs, she waited by his car while he put her luggage in the boot, then reluctantly she got in the passenger's side while he held the door open for her. As he made his way around to the driver's side, her nose crinkled in distaste. Cheryle's perfume! She immediately rolled down the window to get rid of the disgusting odour. Had he made love to Cheryle as well? she wondered and winced as a painful jab of jealousy speared her heart.

'There's no need to have your window opened,' Andrew told her as he slipped behind the steering wheel. 'The car has air-conditioning.'

'Of course,' she murmured, reluctantly rolling it up again.

Neither spoke as they whizzed their way up the coast towards his father's place. Jennifer pretended to watch the scene that passed before them with great interest, but in truth she never saw a thing—not the rugged cliffs that climbed from the roaring green seas below, nor the gulls that swooped and swayed in the breezes. Several times she stole little glances at Andrew, but the swine actually seemed to be enjoying himself, humming, actually humming, to the tunes playing on his tapes.

Finally he brought the car to a halt outside a high, chocolate-painted fence. 'This is it,' he said, cheerfully turning towards her. 'Your home for the next couple of weeks.'

Jennifer stared at the high fence. It looked like a prison fence. 'Do you live with your father?' she asked in dread.

Andrew chuckled. 'Nope. But I don't live far from here. When I'm in town I stay at my shack further up the coast.' His arm stretched across the back of the seat to rest on her shoulders. 'Disappointed?' he asked in a roguish manner.

Jennifer shrugged away from him, giving him a disdainful glance. 'Relieved is the word,' she said scathingly.

Again he chuckled. 'I usually have dinner with Dad, though,' he continued smoothly, 'and afterwards, either a quick game of Scrabble or we sit and watch a show on television.' He smiled encouragingly. 'So you'll be seeing plenty of me while you're here,' he said, reaching across to open her door. 'Won't that be nice, mm?'

'Words wouldn't describe,' she shrugged, making no move to step out of the car. 'I wish I hadn't allowed you to talk me into this,' she said, then laughed bitterly. 'But of course you didn't talk me into it . . . you forced me to come here. I should have brought my own car. At least then I could have stopped home on my way here to water my plants.'

'We can stop and water your plants whenever you wish,' he told her, his fingers moving up the slender column of her neck to trail through her silken tresses. She shivered and shut her eyes, and when she opened them Andrew was watching her, a disturbing smile touching the corners of his mouth. Jennifer blinked against the light shining from his eyes, and made to move away from him, but found she couldn't. Helplessly she looked up at him. 'I ... I don't like being a guest in someone's home. I never feel comfortable.'

'Maybe not, but at least you'll be safe. Anyway, I think you'll find Dad a gracious host, and Mary, his housekeeper, will adore having you to fuss over.'

Andrew led her to the gate and swung it open. When the gate clicked shut behind her, she felt as a small animal must, when it knows it has been trapped!

CHAPTER NINE

JENNIFER reluctantly allowed Andrew to steer her through the beautifully landscaped gardens surrounding his father's home. The house was a cream brick structure with a wide patio extending out towards the pool which was nestled in a corner of the garden. The old man lounged in a chair beside the pool, and Andrew's hand gave Jennifer's a warning squeeze as he half dragged her towards his father.

The old man looked up, and she experienced shock at his frail appearance. His hair was just as white, but all the vitality she had remembered him having had all but disappeared. But as he smiled and spoke there was the same gentleness of manner, and she relaxed, warming towards him immediately.

'Ah, Jennifer,' he greeted her, extending his hand to clasp one of her own. 'Andrew said he was bringing you for a visit, and I was beginning to think you weren't coming after all.' He smiled at them both, his eyes resting on the suitcase Andrew was holding.

Andrew put the suitcase down. 'Jennifer will be staying for a while, Dad. She's been overdoing it lately and needs someone to keep an eye on her.'

'Tut, tut, tut,' the old man wagged a finger at her. 'Well, you've come to the right place, young lady. Mary will see you don't lift a finger, and I spend practically all my time dozing in the sun. No one will bother you here.'

Jennifer murmured her thanks, her cheeks flushing with embarrassment at Andrew's explanation of why she was here. But apparently the old man didn't know much about what was happening at the Agency, and for this she was grateful. She watched as Andrew made his father more comfortable in his chair, her eyes falling on the two walking canes which leaned against it.

'That's much better,' the old man sighed gratefully, his lids drooping. 'Now see that the young lady gets settled and tell Mary to cook something special for dinner. None of that boiled stuff she seems to think I'm so fond of!'

Jennifer's mouth twitched into a smile. The old man obviously hadn't lost his spirit. Andrew straightened and looked at her, a mischievous glint in his eyes. 'Dad has to be watched like a hawk,' he grinned. 'He's on a special diet which means all his food has to be poached or boiled—pretty boring, I know, but it's for his own good.'

They slipped quietly away from the dozing gentleman so he didn't hear what his son had to say. As they made their way towards the house Jennifer agreed. 'Yes, my auntie was like that. She knew she wasn't allowed to have ice cream, but whenever she thought no one was watching she would sneak some out of the freezer. The funny part of it was, up until she knew she couldn't have it, she never liked it.'

'That's a woman for you,' Andrew laughed.

'Contrary all the time!' He smiled down at her. 'Dad's not as bad as that. Not once have we found him lurking in front of the freezer or hiding lollies under his pillow.'

'Lollies?' she joined him in his laughter. 'My auntie never hid lollies under her pillow.'

'No? Mine did. Aunt Bertha, the peppermint lady—that's what I used to call her when I was a kid. I remember she always smelled like peppermints. Her hair, her clothes . . .'

'Her sheets, her pillowcases, her blankets,' Jennifer laughed in delight, finishing his sentence for him.

'She was a dear old thing,' Andrew mused. 'Old age robs us of people just when they start to become interesting.'

'Yes,' she sighed, 'I know what you mean. Whenever our family gathers for the holidays, invariably the conversation drifts to what our dear old aunts and uncles, or our grandparents, used to say or do. You can never forget them and you never want to.' She cast him a sideways glance. 'But I don't think they become interesting just when they're old. I think you only find them interesting when you become older yourself. You know,' she flushed under his amused glance, 'you seem to appreciate them more, can begin to understand the wisdom of their ways.'

'Like taking ice cream from the freezer and hiding lollies under a pillow?' His brows were raised in a mockingly innocent gesture.

'In a way,' she answered slowly, not rising to the bait. 'Doing things like that is only a side effect of old age. I suppose it's a last desperate bid for independence.' She looked up at him. 'Sad, isn't it? We'll be like that some day.'

He considered this. 'I think I'll go for something a little more substantial than ice cream or peppermints, though. Whisky would be nice—a flask of whisky under my pillow.'

Mary greeted them at the door, smiling broadly. Andrew offered the same explanation about why Jennifer was there, and Jennifer was immediately taken under the housekeeper's wing. The housekeeper was a woman in her fifties, Jennifer guessed, and when she was being shown to her room Mary told her she had worked for Adam Thorpe for almost twenty years.

'Unpack your things,' said Mary. 'If you want to rest, go ahead. There won't be any restrictions here.'

'Thanks,' Jennifer murmured, starting to feel guilty about the attention she was receiving under false pretences.

With Mary gone, Jennifer looked around her room. It was a very pleasant room, she decided, with its white cane furniture, pink curtains and bedspread and tasteful wallpaper. There was a connecting bathroom with the same colour scheme. She wandered over to the large picture window where she had a good view of the pool and gardens.

Andrew was with his father, helping him across the lawn. Matt had once told her that Adam Thorpe had married late in life and Andrew was his only child. Mrs Thorpe had died in tragic

circumstances, a boating accident, when Andrew
was still a baby. As she watched Andrew with his
father she was struck, as she had been upon their
arrival, by Andrew's devotion to the grand old
man. She smiled, wondering how a gentle, softly
spoken person could have fathered such a wild,
untamed creature as Andrew! Perhaps he took
after his mother, she thought as she turned away
from the window to start her unpacking.

Lifting up her suitcase, she put it on the bed and
opened it, taking out her garments. She began
slowly, then worked in feverish dismay. Andrew
had packed everything *except* her office clothes!
There were jeans, slacks, shorts, tops and
undergarments. He had even thought to pack a
few bikinis. Everything except what she needed
most—her working outfits.

She fought down her panic. Andrew wouldn't
have done it deliberately, she reasoned. He knew
she had to go to work, he probably planned on
driving her home tomorrow to pick up the rest of
her things. Then she remembered she had had two
suitcases. The other was still in the car. Perhaps he
had packed her things separately in that. But no,
that suitcase was too small. It only housed her
toiletries.

Fighting her ever-increasing sense of uneasiness,
Jennifer put away her things, arranging everything
neatly in the drawers. With her unpacking done
she wondered what she should do next. She
couldn't very well be expected to remain in her
room, but she didn't much care for the idea of
wandering aimlessly about the house. She fell

across the bed, miserable for allowing herself to be placed in such an awkward situation.

The bedroom door opened and Andrew sauntered in. 'Well, well,' he drawled, seeing her on the bed. 'Glad to see you're waiting for me!'

She sat up quickly, swinging her legs over the side. 'You forgot to pack most of my clothes,' she accused him.

He looked at the empty suitcase on the floor. 'You're only here for a short while, not for ever!'

'Thank God for that!' Jennifer remarked rather tightly. 'I love your father and I rather suspect Mary will smother me with kindness. It's only the son that worries me.'

He chuckled, crossing over to sit next to her on the bed. She jumped up immediately, not trusting him to behave himself.

'My, but you're a jumpy, skittish little thing,' he mocked her, lying back on the bed with his arms folded under his head. 'Why don't you change into one of those skimpy little bikinis and we'll go for a swim.'

She gaped at him. He fully expected her to change in front of him, and she could tell he had no intention of leaving.

'Why are you in my room?' she asked him.

His eyes wandered insolently down her body. 'Just checking to see if you need anything.'

She swung away from him. 'Don't be crude,' she half-whispered. She heard him spring to his feet, then felt his hands on her shoulders turning her around. Her eyes were drawn to his and her heart caught in her throat at the sight of his smile. But she stood still, staring up at him with a sort of breathless determination, willing herself not to be affected by his touch or his smile. 'I want to go home,' she tilted. 'I have no wish to stay here.'

A glacial hardness settled in his eyes and his hands gripped cruelly into the soft flesh of her shoulders. 'Miss him already, do you?' he grated.

She didn't cringe under the pressure of his hands. She cringed when she saw the bitterness in his eyes, heard it from his lips. Of course he meant Kevin.

'The reason doesn't matter,' she answered wearily.

Andrew's hands dropped from her shoulders. 'It doesn't fit in with my plans to take you home. You're here now and here you will stay!'

'What about my clothes? I haven't any clothes to wear to work on Monday. If you're busy, lend me your car and I'll go back and get something.'

A smile spread slowly across his face. 'There's no need.'

Jennifer shrugged her impatience. 'Be reasonable,' she snapped. 'I can't very well show up for work dressed in jeans or a pair of shorts.'

'You won't be turning up at all!' She heard the satisfaction in his voice, saw it in his eyes.

'Wh-what do you mean?' she stammered.

'Matt will be back on Monday—he's getting bored at home. Now it's your turn for a few days off.'

She stared at the look of smug arrogance on his hateful features. 'You planned this, didn't you?' she hissed. Her fists came up and pummelled his chest, but he pushed her hands aside as if they were mere feathers.

'Yes, I guess I did,' he admitted, looking enormously pleased with himself.

'But why?' she pleaded, tears springing to her eyes. 'Can you tell me why you . . . you *tricked* me?'

When he didn't answer, the reason came to her in a rush. She took a step backward, her fist at her mouth, knuckles showing white.

'But of course,' she whispered, her eyes wide with hurt. 'It will be easier for you to spy on me here, won't it? Just tell me one thing. Are Mary and . . . and your father in on this too? Have they both received their instructions on how to treat a criminal?' Her eyes flew to the telephone on the little white night-table. 'Is that thing bugged?' she asked, sarcasm replacing the hurt. 'Is the room wired for sound? How about Kevin? What if he tries to reach me? Will I be permitted to speak with him for a few minutes each day, or will he be told I'm not available?'

His eyes narrowed dangerously as he watched her, his hands thrust in his jeans pockets. Enraged, Jennifer flew to the mirror hanging above the dressing table. 'Is this a two-way mirror?' she sobbed, tears of helpless outrage streaming down her cheeks. She whirled to face him, her shoulders hunched. 'You'll never believe that I had nothing to do with those thefts. You plan to persecute me, torture me until in desperation I confess to something I never did!' She squared her shoulders and wiped away her tears. a wan smile lifting the corners of her mouth. 'Well, it won't work—you said so yourself. There's nothing meek or downtrodden about *me*!' she flared in a bold rush of defiance and a determined tilt to her pert little chin.

Andrew let out his breath in a tired sigh, taking the few steps necessary to reach her. 'Now that you've finished your little tantrum,' he told her smoothly, 'you can get ready for dinner.' He walked towards the door. 'Don't forget to wash your face and hands,' he tossed over his shoulder. 'They're grubby!'

She picked up a hairbrush and flung it at his retreating figure, only to miss and watch it land on the carpet. Frantic lashes swept down to hide her fear as he turned to look down at the brush and then across to her. During her outburst Andrew had looked fierce, but now the scowl cleared and a teasing light sparked a new glow in his eyes.

'You can't seem to do anything right,' he murmured sympathetically, then she heard him chuckle softly as he shut the door behind him.

She would have liked to have worn a dress to dinner, but thanks to Andrew this wasn't possible. Still, she had to look presentable, and after carefully examining what little she had she finally decided on a pair of pink slacks and white tailored shirt. Brushing her hair until her scalp tingled, she put the brush down and stared at her reflection in the mirror. But she didn't see the shining blonde hair, or the perfect oval of her face. She wasn't even struck by the deeply troubled eyes, dark pools of green surrounded by their thick fringe.

All she could think of was how Andrew had

tricked her, pretending to be concerned about her safety when all he was after was revenge. She wondered how he planned to keep her here with only a frail old man and a housekeeper as her guards. Presumably he would go to work on Monday, and when he did, she would make her escape. The house wasn't in a secluded area, there were neighbours on both sides. She would merely ring for a taxi and leave.

Ten minutes later she dragged herself from her room and made her way towards the chattering sounds coming from the dining room. Andrew and his father were standing with drinks in their hands and the old man greeted her fondly as she stepped into the room. She avoided the piercing glance that Andrew shot her and refused his offer of a drink.

Dinner was a strained affair and several times she was aware of the old man's anxiety as she pecked uninterestedly at her food. Only Andrew seemed to be enjoying himself, chatting his way happily through the various courses. It was a great relief when Mary finally cleared away the remains of the dessert and she was was finally able to leave.

She stood up from the table and addressed the old man. 'Thank you,' she said. 'That was delicious, but no coffee for me, thanks. I think I'll retire to my room and do a bit of reading.' She turned stiffly to Andrew, who was watching her with undisguised amusement. 'I trust you'll be returning to your shack shortly for a well earned rest?'

Unaware of the animosity that slithered between

his son and Jennifer, at her words, the old man smiled. 'No, Andrew will spend the night here,' he said. 'He's promised me a game of Scrabble, haven't you son?'

Andrew pushed himself away from the table and stood up, his movement effectively silencing the words of protest that hovered on Jennifer's parted lips.

'That's right, Dad,' he agreed, walking around to help his father up from the table. 'Care to join us?' he asked Jennifer as she remained rooted to the spot. 'We wouldn't mind,' he assured her, smiling benevolently at her stiff attitude. 'Would we, Dad?'

'No, thanks,' she answered icily, a frozen smile on her lips. She moved towards the door. 'Goodnight,' she offered before fleeing from the room and bolting her door behind her as she went into her bedroom. So, she fumed, Andrew had lied to her about sleeping at his shack. He had planned all along to remain here at his father's house, to watch over her, no doubt. Was there any end to his trickery? she wondered dismally as she prepared herself for bed. Her small case containing her toiletries had been placed in her room and she rummaged around in it until she found her night cream.

Finally in bed, she prepared for a sleepless night. It seemed more important than ever to escape from Andrew's clutches—just for spite, if for no other reason, she thought sleepily, the day's events finally catching up with her as her eyes slowly closed.

The next afternoon, Andrew drove her and his father to his shack for a barbecue. His 'shack' turned out to be a huge house nestled on the clifftops overlooking the roaring surf below. Native trees and shrubs cluttered the grounds and had been allowed to grow in wild confusion. Parrots and cockatoos screeched and squawked while a pair of kookaburras laughed in the trees. It seemed a lonely place, and inside there was barely any furniture except for essentials.

The place was exactly what Jennifer had imagined Andrew would have. Its starkness and harshness suited him. There was also a strange, haunting beauty which seemed to reach out and touch her. She loved it!

'Do you like it?' Andrew asked her after showing her around.

'Yes,' she answered simply, her face showing her delight.

Andrew let out his breath as though her answer had not only pleased him but had offered him relief as well. He took her hand and raised it to his lips, pressing his mouth against her palm, but she snatched the hand away as if it had been burnt. The old man sauntered towards them, and as Andrew settled his father in a chair, Jennifer smiled warmly at the elderly gentleman, grateful that he was there.

Mary had packed almost everything, except for the steaks. Andrew got these from his house, and when Jennifer saw the size of them she was afraid most of hers would be wasted. But when Andrew handed her a steak platter with her steak cooked to a turn, her mouth watered and she ate every morsel.

While Andrew cleaned the barbecue, Jennifer and the old man fed scraps of bread roll, celery, lettuce and fruit to the birds, both of them laughing at the bird's antics and scolding them for their greediness. Several times Jennifer called out to Andrew to watch this or that and he would stop what he was doing and smile at her exuberance, a smile which she sometimes found very disturbing.

The old man tired easily, so it was necessary to return before dusk. As they drove out of the long, twisting driveway Jennifer turned her head back to look at the house. She felt sad leaving it somehow; it was indeed such a lonely place. She sighed and turned her head back and caught Andrew's glance. Their eyes fused together and with a start she realised he had read her mind. Flushing deeply, she bowed her head and rode in silence back to the old man's place.

When she woke up the next morning, she quickly showered and dressed. The old man had already had breakfast and Andrew had left for work. She could go now. Who would stop her? But it seemed so rude just to pack up and go. Her quarrel was with Andrew, not with his father or Mary. His father had treated her like a favourite daughter instead of a guest and Mary had fussed over her just as Andrew had predicted she would.

So by lunchtime she was still there, having spent the morning chatting and playing Scrabble with the old man and helping Mary in the kitchen. After lunch the old man retired to his room for a nap and Mary sat in front of the television to view her serials, which she never missed, she explained to Jennifer.

'I think I'll go into town,' Jennifer heard herself saying, then braced herself for Mary's flat explanations of why she couldn't or shouldn't go.

Mary looked up from her programme and smiled. 'All right, dear. Dinner will be at six.'

Jennifer gaped at her. 'You mean ... I can go? You don't mind?'

'Of course not. You're a guest here, you can come and go as you please. I certainly don't expect you to sit around and watch these silly old programmes.'

'It was just that I thought Andrew would mind.' She looked at Mary closely. 'He didn't say anything to you about ... about keeping me here, did he?'

Mary looked at her in surprise and then laughed. 'Good heavens, dear, why would he do that?'

'I don't know,' mumbled Jennifer, feeling foolish. 'I just thought he might have.' She took a deep breath. 'I think I'll go, then.'

While she got ready, she decided what she must do. She would go to the Agency and manage to persuade Andrew to go with her to see Kevin. Kevin could convince him once and for all that she and Kevin weren't involved in any sinister plots to destroy the Agency. If anything were to develop from their relationship then first she must remove all traces of doubt.

Pleased with her decision and line of action,

Jennifer rang for a taxi, and when it came bade Mary a fond farewell, promising to be back for dinner by six.

But Andrew had already left by the time she got to the Agency. It was near closing time and no one seemed to know where he was. Cheryle wasn't at her desk, and Jennifer was told that she had left with Andrew. Sickened to the core, she made it into her office, where she leaned against her desk. Her mind whirled in dizzy confusion while she worked her way around the desk to sink into her chair. It all became suddeny clear. Andrew had dumped her at his father's house to get rid of her while he worked his charms on Cheryle. Obviously, she had become an embarrassment to him, criticising him for the extended lunch hours he had taken with Cheryle. The cad!

Pain seared her heart and she thought she would die. There was a light tap on her door and she looked up to see one of the junior artists standing there with some sketches in his hands. He crossed over and put it on her desk, saying something, but she didn't hear. She was barely aware when he left, her eyes staring blindly down at the sketches. Finally she got up and carried them to Matt's office, kneeling to open the safe. When she opened the door, the unmistakable odour of Cheryle's perfume reached out to her nostrils. Slowly, realisation hit her. She pulled out the campaign with Cheryle's perfume on it. The scent was on every sheet. She put back the campaign and locked the safe. Like a sleepwalker she made her way to Cheryle's desk.

She opened every drawer until she found what she was looking for—a miniature camera! Cheryle was the inside contact! Jennifer's eyes fell on Cheryle's desk diary. Her icy fingers flicked through the pages, stopping several times as she examined the entries. Finally she snapped the book shut. It was all there—Kevin's initials, times and dates. Andrew had been half right; Kevin was involved all right, but with Cheryle, not herself.

Jennifer could never remember afterwards how she got from the office to Kevin's place. She had vague recollections of a taxi driver, but that was all. She stumbled up to Kevin's flat and pounded on the door. When it was opened and she saw him there, she burst into tears. It seemed four years of a trusted friendship had been nothing more than a mockery, a cruel joke. She cried, not for him as he was now, but for the young man of those years ago who had confided in her all his hopes and plans for the future.

She wanted to reach out and touch him. Her heart broke for him because now he had no future. 'Oh, Kevin!' she cried brokenly, flinging her arms around him in a smothering embrace, clutching at him the way a mother would when finally faced with the truth about a trusted son. But it seemed fate hadn't finished with Jennifer yet. As she held Kevin's face in her hands, trying desperately to reach what might have made him turn to a life of crime, Andrew dragged her from him.

He had been in the lounge room, but she wasn't to know that. Recognising her voice, he had come to check for himself. He had Cheryle by the arm and behind them both was the new doorman. The doorman took Kevin's arm and Jennifer realised, as he did, that he must be a detective. Andrew had obviously planted him to spy on her. No wonder he knew of her activities!

Everything happened quickly after that, and Jennifer watched in a state of numbed shock as the detective prepared to take Kevin and Cheryle away. Her confused mind took in snatches of information. Apparently Andrew and the detective had decided the time was right to close in on the pair and make the arrests.

Kevin cast her a glance and she reponded to his obvious misery, her eyes filled with pain. Andrew caught the look that passed between her and Kevin and a deep flush spread menacingly across his cheeks. He crossed over to where she stood. 'Why didn't you stay at Dad's?' he grated.

She blinked up at him and shook her head. There seemed no point in telling him now. She heard him suck in his breath.

'Forget him,' he rasped. 'He's not worthy of your love.'

She bowed her head. 'He's still a person, worthy of my concern.'

His hand was far from gentle as he cupped her chin, forcing her head up to meet the smouldering black coals of his eyes. The clear green of her eyes were deep with misery.

'Those eyes,' he murmured as though speaking to himself, 'I thought they told me so much!' She saw pain briefly sear his own, before he dropped his hand from her chin. 'And to think I was entertaining thoughts of asking you to marry me,' he added bitterly, thrusting his hands in his pockets. 'I would have begged, had I thought it would do any good!'

Then he was gone. Gone! *Gone!*

CHAPTER TEN

AN uneasy peace settled around the Agency. Andrew called a meeting early the next morning, explaining, without going into too much detail, that the thieves had been caught and that new security measures would soon be introduced. A new girl was hired to replace Cheryle, and by the end of the week things had settled down to such an extent that it was hard to believe anything out of the ordinary had ever taken place.

Hard to believe, that was, for everyone except for Jennifer. She had been completely shattered. As though the events leading up to Kevin's and Cheryle's arrests hadn't been enough, to find out from Andrew that he had been about to ask her to marry him had been in itself earth-shattering.

She tormented herself with the knowledge she had nobody to blame but herself. That she loved him desperately and had botched everything up filled her with blind despair. If only she hadn't left his father's place, then she wouldn't be in this hopeless situation that she now found herself in.

Several times she considered ringing her parents, but they were so far away there was nothing they could do to help. She longed for a shoulder to cry on, a sympathetic ear to listen to her heartbroken cries of despair.

Andrew treated her with disdainful scorn. He

ignored her at meetings and treated anything she had to say with bored contempt. The only times he actually spoke to her was when he gave her work. He piled it on as if she was some sort of machine or robot, snapping and snarling orders at her as if she had no feelings at all.

Never once did she object. In fact she didn't trust herself to speak to him. He hated her, this she knew; it was apparent by his every look, his every gesture. She bowed under his scathing glances, flinched under his sarcastic remarks. She longed to run after him, explain to him that she didn't love Kevin, that she only cared for him the way a stronger human being cares for a weaker one.

But he gave her no opportunity and she didn't know how to seek one. At times she was plagued with the gnawing ache that perhaps it was Cheryle he loved and that he hadn't loved her at all. He had been dating Cheryle; it must have been a severe jolt to find out she was involved with the thefts.

Plagued by doubts and fears, somehow Jennifer lived through the week, hardly aware when one day ended and another began. Even the fact that the junior artists had come up with a brilliant display of workmanship did nothing to boost her ego. Andrew brought it to her and tossed it on her desk.

'The Corser people have accepted this,' he snapped, his voice grating. 'Well, aren't you going to look at it?' he snarled when she didn't give it a glance. Her shoulders shook under his wrath and her hands trembled when she reached out to touch the pages. He swore loudly and snatched it away.

'Never mind,' he sneered. 'Obviously you have other, more important things on your mind.' He turned to leave. 'You'll be pleased to learn Kevin has been granted bail. I arranged it for him because I couldn't bear to watch you pining for him any longer. So why don't you get out of here and go see him?' The door slammed after him.

She stared after him, watching the closed door as if he still stood there. He wants me to leave, she thought. He can't bear the sight of me. She had thought before he was trying to break her, it had never occurred to her that he wanted her out of the business.

Several times she caught Matt watching her, pity in his eyes. Was her heartbreak so obvious that even Matt could see how she felt, was feeling, and would feel for ever? She would never leave. Sleepless nights led to loss of appetite. Dark smudges appeared under her eyes. She became jittery, but still she held on, determined that in this instance at least, she would not be beaten.

Finally, it was Matt who intervened. He called Jennifer into his office early one morning. 'What's going on?' he asked her, as soon as she had taken a chair.

'What do you mean?' she hedged.

'Between you and Andrew. Don't pretend you don't know,' he sighed, leaning heavily against the back of his chair. He eyed her critically. 'You're a bag of bones! You look a mess!'

'Gee, thanks,' she muttered. 'Just what every girl longs to hear.'

'Now don't get cute with me. We've always been

straight with each other and I want some straight answers now. I repeat, what's going on?'

Jennifer turned her head away. Matt was a dear, but there was truly nothing he could do to help. 'Nothing,' she answered miserably.

Matt sighed. 'I've seen the way Andrew's been treating you, the work he's channelled your way. I've spoken to him about it, but he as good as warned me to mind my own business, but don't think you're going to do the same.' He hunched forward, folding his big, beefy arms on his desk. 'Andrew might be running this show, but don't forget, I'm still your boss. He shouldn't be giving you extra work without checking with me first.'

'I suppose he has his reasons for what he's doing,' Jennifer owned reluctantly. 'But none of my regular work has suffered, Matt. I've been able to cope.'

'Cope?' he spluttered. 'Haven't you been listening, girl? You're a wreck. You look sick. What time was it you left the office last night?'

'I . . . I don't know. Not very late.'

'Well, I know—I checked with Security this morning. You didn't leave until after nine o'clock. It was the same the night before and the night before.' He slammed his burly fist against the desk. 'This has got to stop.' He reached for his phone. 'I should have done this ages ago,' he muttered.

'Who are you calling?' asked Jennifer. 'Not Andrew, I hope?'

'Yes, Andrew. I'm going to get him up here and get some sense out of the two of you.'

'Matt! Don't—please!' she gasped, sitting upright in her chair, her eyes rounded in horror.

Matt slowly hung up the phone. 'This is even more serious than I thought,' he said, while Jennifer sat back in her chair, almost shaking with relief. 'You love him, don't you.' It was a flat statement and she knew it would be silly to deny it.

'Yes,' she whispered, rapidly blinking her eyes to hold back the tears.

'You don't look like a girl who's in love,' Matt stated the obvious. 'Have things changed so much over the years that this is how a girl in love looks and acts?'

She attempted a smile, but somehow it wouldn't come.

'Does Andrew love you?' Matt asked gently.

Jennifer shook her head. 'He hates me,' she answered tonelessly.

Matt let out a low whistle. Obviously he thought he was getting somewhere. 'Is that why he's been piling all the extra work on to you?' he asked. 'Because he hates you, as you say?'

'Yes.'

He placed the tips of his fingers together, quietly studying her. 'You don't think there could be any other reason?'

She shook her head. 'No. He's trying to get me to quit.'

'If that were so, wouldn't it be better for him just to fire you? After all, he is in charge of the place. I wouldn't be able to stop him.'

'That would be too easy. He . . . he wants to see me suffer.'

Matt smiled. 'And so you're suffering . . . just as he wants you to?'

'I'm not doing it on purpose, if that's what you mean.' Some of the old fire crept back into her voice, pleasing him. 'I suppose if I had any sense, I'd walk out of this place and never come back.'

'Well, you've always had plenty of sense before,' Matt drawled. 'Surely you still have some left.'

'Not any more, I'm afraid. Otherwise I'd be sitting at some other job right now.'

'But then Andrew wouldn't be at some other job, would he? How long do you think you can take this treatment without ending up with a nervous breakdown?'

'Oh, Matt, don't be silly. I'm not the type to have nervous breakdowns.'

'No? Well, I am, and if you and Andrew don't patch up this silly quarrel, that's exactly what I will be having. What with you moping around the place and him snapping and snarling and biting everyone's heads off, it's a miracle we have any staff left. I swear, if he wasn't the old man's son and if I didn't love you like a daughter, I'd fire you both!'

For the first time in weeks, Jennifer smiled. 'I wasn't aware Andrew was behaving so badly,' she said.

'I don't see how you could have missed it,' returned Matt. 'You hardly take your eyes off him.'

Her cheeks coloured and Matt gave himself a silent word of approval. 'Have I been so obvious?' she asked. 'I hope no one else has noticed.'

'Of course everyone's noticed. How could they help doing otherwise? Both of you are putting on quite a show, you know. None of us dare breathe when you and Andrew are in the same room—him prowling around like an angry old lion; you pussyfooting around him like a terrified kitten!'

Jennifer's cheeks were scarlet. 'Oh dear!' she exclaimed, deeply embarrassed. 'How dreadful! I had no idea I was behaving so . . . so . . .'

'So weakly?' Matt supplied the word.

She nodded. 'Something like that,' she admitted reluctantly. 'Oh, Matt, what am I to do? The situation is so hopeless. I'm eating my heart out for a man who hates me, who treats me like dirt under his feet. But I can't leave the job. I've got to be where I can see him, hear his voice, be near him, even if it's only to receive his abuse.' She bowed her head, looking down at her hands. 'I know you must think I'm mad, but I can't help it.'

'Does he have any idea how you feel about him?' Matt asked.

She shook her head. 'He thinks I love Kevin.'

'You're joking! How in tarnation would Andrew get an idea like that into his head?'

'The night they took Kevin away . . . I felt so sorry for him . . . I told Andrew I cared for Kevin.'

'He mistook pity for love?'

'Yes.' The single word was a sob.

'And you haven't told him differently?' Matt asked in disbelief.

She shook her head. 'What would be the use? You've seen the way he treats me. Besides, he was dating Cheryle . . .' She wrung her hands in despair, her eyes full of misery as she gazed across at him.

Matt coughed and stood up from his desk. 'Tomorrow is Saturday,' he said. 'Why don't you take a drive up the coast to Andrew's place? You're both adults, behave like adults. Tell him what you've told me and I'll guarantee he'll explain why he was dating Cheryle. Now, if you don't mind, young lady, I've got work to do. I can't waste any more time discussing your problems.'

Jennifer stood up, the corners of her mouth lifting in a smile. 'Thanks, Matt,' she said gratefully. 'I really do love you.'

'Humph! Don't tell Andrew, then. I don't think I could stand any more of his jealous outbursts.'

'Nor could I,' she chuckled, slipping from Matt's office.

Early the next morning she showered and dressed in a pair of white shorts and pale green top. She pulled her hair back and secured it with a scarf, the same colour as her top. Her green eyes were aglow with excitement and dread. However this meeting with Andrew turned out, nothing could be worse than what she had just lived through. She got her little Morris out of the garage and minutes later she was whizzing up the coastal road leading to Andrew's place.

The kookaburras were laughing in the treetops and the parrots were screeching for food. Apart from the birds, the place seemed deserted. Jennifer parked her car under one of the giant umbrella trees, then walked slowly towards the sprawling bungalow. She knocked several times on the back door before deciding to follow the verandah around to the front.

The front of the house overlooked the ocean. The wide wooden verandah jutted over the cliff to offer a sweeping view of the sand and surf below. From here she could see Andrew, a solitary figure on a lonely stretch of beach. She could have gone down to him. There were steps leading to the beach, but a plan was taking shape in her mind.

Reluctant to take her eyes off him, she watched him for a further few minutes, saw him break into a jog. On the distant horizon there was an ocean liner, and Andrew climbed on some rocks, his hands shading his eyes as he watched it.

With a last lingering glance, Jennifer turned and went into the house, a grin spreading hesitantly across her face. She didn't find a Wedgwood dinner set, nor did she find any crystal. The cutlery was only stainless steel, not heavy silver like her own. The tablecloths were well used, certainly not suitable, but from the linen closet she found a set of sheets which had never been used—hideous things really, with a wild array of purple, orange and green flowers. Jennifer spread one of the sheets across the kitchen table and in the centre she placed a wine bottle. Outside, she gathered some pretty wild flowers and dropped them into the bottle. From the kitchen cupboard she managed to find some matching plates and saucers, but no cups. She searched, and then her eyes fell on the dishwasher. Pulling open the door, she saw he hadn't emptied it and that there were clean cups inside.

With the table finally set to her satisfaction, Jennifer turned her attention to their meal. First she squeezed some oranges, pouring the juice into pewter mugs and putting them in the fridge, taking out bacon and eggs before shutting the door. The eggs were frying, the bacon sizzling and the coffee perking, when she remembered there had to be music! She quickly scampered into the living room, with its beamed ceiling and stone fireplace, to put some records on the stereo.

When she heard Andrew enter the house, she grabbed a tea-towel and tied it around her waist. When he walked into the kitchen her back was facing him and she was humming softly. Her eyes registered no surprise when she turned and saw him leaning against the doorframe. Only her heart quickened its pace at the incredibly handsome picture he made. He was naked except for his black bathing trunks and with a red towel slung over one shoulder. His hair was still damp from his swim and the black hair on his chest formed tiny ringlets against the deep tan of his skin.

'Enjoy your swim?' she asked casually, as though this was what she generally asked him each morning while she fixed their breakfast.

His eyes were alight with amusement. 'Yes, the water was great,' he answered, matching her tone.

'And your jog?' she asked sweetly, flipping eggs on to their plates.

'Especially the jog,' he grinned, watching her every move.

'Didn't that ocean liner look magnificent against the horizon?' she enthused. 'I had a great view of it from your verandah,' she continued, adding bacon to their plates.

'I watched it from the far end of the beach,' he told her, as she passed by him to get the orange juice from the fridge.

'Yes, from the rocks. I thought you looked rather lonely standing there by yourself.' She smiled, kicking the door of the fridge shut with her foot. 'Were you lonely?'

Andrew took the pewter mugs from her hands and placed them on the table, then his hands were on her shoulders and the grin was gone from his face. 'Yes,' he answered softly, his eyes searching her face, 'I was lonely, very lonely.'

'I ... I know,' she whispered, swallowing hard. 'I could tell.'

His hands tightened on her shoulders and she felt her senses weakening as she stared up at him, hungrily devouring every line in his face. 'Can you tell that I love you?' he asked her quietly, his eyes burning into hers with an intensity she had never known before. She shook her head, bewilderment clouding her eyes.

'No ... yes. I don't know.' Her eyes searched his. 'Do you?' she asked hopefully.

Anger smouldered briefly in his eyes and a ragged sigh tore from his lips. He jerked his head towards the table. 'Are you hungry?' he asked, then, not waiting for an answer, led her from the kitchen. 'Breakfast can wait,' he rasped, 'but not us. We've waited long enough as it is.'

He took her into the living room and sat beside her on the soft leather-bound sofa. Taking her hands in his, he kissed each fingertip and then her palms. 'Let's start with Kevin,' he said, his eyes watching her closely. 'Do you love him?'

'No!' she answered truthfully, then added. 'I never have. He's always been . . . just a friend.'

'And now he's a friend in need, is that it? Despite what he's done to you?'

'Yes. I'm sorry, Andrew, but I just can't turn my back on him.'

'All right,' he sighed, 'I suppose I'm going to have to accept that, no matter how distasteful I find it.'

'You asked me about Kevin,' she began quietly, 'so now I must ask you about Cheryle.'

His brows arched in surprise. 'Cheryle?' he queried. 'What has she got to do with us?'

'Well, you dated her . . . often. You must care for her,' she told him unhappily.

His short, loud bark of laughter startled her. 'Care for her? You've got to be kidding! Cheryle's nothing but a common little tramp.'

Jennifer's eyes registered her surprise. 'But you paid so much attention to her. Those yellow roses . . . they were so beautiful.'

'Those roses were meant for you, and if you'd stopped to think for a minute, you would have realised they were exactly the same colour as the one I brought you the morning I fixed *you* breakfast.' His hand swept down her head and unfastened the scarf binding her hair. 'The palest gold,' he murmured, watching as her hair slipped through his fingers.

'But Cheryle said you'd given them to her,'

Jennifer insisted, trying to ignore the sensations Andrew's hand on her neck was causing, but determined they should clear up all mysteries before they could expect to understand the mystery of their hearts, and how his merest touch could send her own racing.

'I gathered that, when you came to see me,' he said, watching her hair cascade through his fingers, the light from the window catching each strand and making it appear like shimmering gold.

'Well, why didn't you tell me?' she asked, deliberately moving away from him so he couldn't reach her, anger blazing in her eyes.

Andrew chuckled. 'You look like a little kitten ready to scratch my eyes out.' His eyes mocked her. 'Were you jealous?'

She looked away from him, gathering up her legs to lean her chin on her knees. 'Terribly!' she muttered.

'Good,' he surprised her by saying, 'Now you know how I felt about you and Kevin.'

Her eyes flew to his face. 'You were jealous of Kevin?' she asked incredulously.

'Terribly!' he muttered.

A delighted smile danced along her lips. 'Good!' she chuckled, laughter shining in her eyes. 'But you haven't told me why you allowed me to think the flowers were for Cheryle.'

He had been watching her with amusement, but now he grew suddenly serious. 'I suspected almost from the beginning that Cheryle was involved with the thefts.' He smiled when he saw a disbelieving look cross Jennifer's features. 'I realise I put you through some pretty hard times, and at first, you were my prime suspect.'

'You put me through hell,' she scowled, remembering. 'How long was I your number one suspect?'

A teasing light shone in his eyes. 'Oh, for about five minutes,' he confessed casually.

'Five minutes? But ... but ...'

Andrew laughed and drew her near, placing her head against his shoulder. 'When I heard what was happening at the Agency, it was logical to conclude that the thief had to be you or Cheryle. Matt was out of the question, I know him too well. I doubt he's taken so much as an elastic band from the place, in all the years he's worked there.' Andrew's lips pressed against her hair and she closed her eyes, listening to him speak. 'The five minutes I suspected you was when you were holding that campaign, but even when I caught you red-handed I couldn't convince myself you were a thief. Cheryle had access to the mail. She opened it each morning for you and Matt. Whenever a new combination for the safe arrived, she merely steamed open the envelope, jotted down the numbers and then sealed it again.'

Jennifer stirred in the crook of his arm, shaking her head in wonder. 'How simple you make it sound,' she said. 'While Matt and I were committing the new combination to memory, Cheryle already had it. You must think we were pretty dumb not to think of that ourselves.'

'Not at all,' he smiled. 'Cheryle was your trusted receptionist and secretary. Sometimes it's difficult to see the forest for the trees. You and Matt are so trusting yourselves, it would never have occurred to either one of you to look under your own noses for the thief.'

Jennifer nodded slowly. 'I suppose you're right,' she agreed, 'but what made you connect Kevin with Cheryle?'

'When you told me Kevin used to work at the Agency. I checked on some old files Dad keeps at his home, and it turned out Cheryle's uncle used to work there as well. Dad dismissed him, apparently for drunkenness. The family put up quite a stink, apparently.'

'So Cheryle was after revenge?' Jennifer digested this. 'Do you think Cheryle was behind those phone calls and that note which was slipped under my door?'

His hand was gentle as he stroked her hair. 'Yes. I checked, and Cheryle was never at Printing the day you received that call in Matt's office. She was minding the switchboard, and knowing you were alone upstairs, put the call through on Matt's line. She also wrote that note, but it was Kevin who stuck it under the door and then removed it from the bureau, when you had him over for dinner.'

Jennifer shivered, leaning against his reassuring warmth. 'I wasn't particularly frightened,' she confessed, 'but it was all rather nerve-racking just the same. I found myself wondering what was to happen next.'

Andrew gathered her in his arms. 'I know,' he whispered against her hair. 'That's why I had Jack planted as the doorman for your block of units. I was in constant touch with him.' His mouth burned a fiery trail down the side of her cheek and when his lips found hers, she responded eagerly, straining towards him, letting him know how much she loved him. He finally released her, his eyes roaming lovingly across her face. 'I thought you loved Kevin,' he said. 'I know it was cruel of me to suggest that you and Kevin were working together, but I wanted you to realise he was working with someone and that the logical person would have to be Cheryle. I wanted you to find out for yourself what a louse he was, but I must admit, when you were so obviously upset about the flowers you thought I'd given Cheryle, I knew I stood a chance.'

Jennifer shook her head in wonder. 'There was never any competition between you and Kevin,' she said, 'but I thought I didn't stand a chance against Cheryle. You were always paying so much attention to her, admiring her perfume, paying her compliments.'

'I only pretended to do those things to gain her confidence,' he said. 'I detested that perfume. I never want to smell it again in my life—but don't you see, my darling, I had to do what I did, because I knew sooner or later she would let things slip. She did, and I was able to build my case against her and Kevin. The flowers only helped.'

Jennifer stared at him. 'Why, that's terrible!' she gasped. 'I've never heard of anything so . . . so . . .' She couldn't think of a word bad enough to describe what Andrew had deliberately set out to do.

'Ruthless?' he supplied, a sardonic gleam in his eye. 'Don't kid yourself. Compared to what I felt like doing to them both, it was mild enough treatment.'

Jennifer knew he spoke the truth. Andrew would not have had any qualms about what he must do, or how he would do it. In everything he had done, she realised now, he had done it for her, from sparing her feelings to saving her life. She looked up at him and he was struck by the love shining from her eyes. The time for criticisms was over, but there was something she felt she must tell him.

'You'll have to smell Cheryle's perfume just one more time,' she told him with an impish grin. 'It's sprinkled over our latest campaign. It must have been on her hands when she was filming it.'

'Matt can take care of it. I won't be there on Monday.'

Her heart stood still as an icy band of fear clutched at it, squeezing out every last drop of blood. 'You won't?' she asked, her voice barely a whisper.

'Nope! Now that everything is settled here, I must get back to my factories in Europe.'

'I see,' she whispered, in that same shocked voice. She turned away from him, so that he might not see the heartbreak in her eyes. 'I ... I realised you would have to go back some day, of course, but I didn't think it would be so soon.' She squeezed her eyes shut, as a small sob tore from her throat. Oh, God, she thought, desperately trying to pull herself together, please give me strength to live through this moment.

'If it had been up to me,' said Andrew, gently

taking her in his arms, 'we would have left much sooner.' He lifted her face and saw the tears.

'We?'

He raised his brows in his typically arrogant fashion. 'Of course. After all I've been through to prove your innocence, you don't think I would leave you behind?'

A smile broke through her tears. 'It would hardly seem reasonable,' she agreed.

'Then you will come with me to Europe . . . as my wife?'

'Is there any other way to travel?' she asked, sheer joy lighting her eyes as he swept her into his arms to hold her against his heart. 'But you'll have to give me some time to get ready. My parents will have to be notified, and then there's Matt. We both just can't leave without finding someone to take my place. Matt will . . .'

'Don't worry about Matt,' he growled, nibbling at her ear. 'He already knows you're going to marry me. I told him when he rang me up last night to tell me you were coming today!'

'Matt *told* you?' gasped Jennifer. 'Why, that old so-and so!' Then she laughed, her eyes sparkling. 'I can't say I'm surprised. Really I'm rather grateful. It softened you up for my visit,' she teased.

'How I love you,' Andrew whispered in her ear. 'I adore you. I can't wait until we're married.' He cupped her face in his hands. 'Tell me you love me,' he commanded her.

'I love you, Andrew,' she whispered softly. 'I've loved only you, for such a long time.'

He knew she meant it. For once he didn't argue!

An epic novel of exotic rituals
and the lure of the Upper Amazon

THE TAKERS RIVER OF GOLD

JERRY AND S.A. AHERN

THE TAKERS are the intrepid Josh Culhane and the seductive Mary Mulrooney. These two adventurers launch an incredible journey into the Brazilian rain forest. Far upriver, the jungle yields its deepest secret—the lost city of the Amazon warrior women!

THE TAKERS series is making publishing history. Awarded *The Romantic Times* first prize for High Adventure in 1984, the opening book in the series was hailed by *The Romantic Times* as "the next trend in romance writing and reading. Highly recommended!"

Jerry and S.A. Ahern have never been better!